THE

Barbara Cartland, ... historian, playwrig... ...ker and television personali.., ...as now written 150 books. She has had a number of historical books published and several biographical ones, including a biography of her brother, Major Ronald Cartland, who was the first Member of Parliament to be killed in the war. The book has a preface by Sir Winston Churchill.

In private life, Miss Cartland, who is a Dame of Grace of St John of Jerusalem, has fought for better conditions and salaries for midwives and nurses. As President of the Royal College of Midwives (Hertfordshire Branch), she has been invested with the first Badge of Office ever given in Great Britain, which was subscribed to by the midwives themselves. She has also championed the cause of old people and gipsies.

Barbara Cartland is deeply interested in vitamin therapy and is President of the National Association for Health.

*By the same author in Pan Books*

THE BORED BRIDEGROOM
THE PENNILESS PEER
THE DANGEROUS DANDY
THE CRUEL COUNT
THE CASTLE OF FEAR

*Please see page 217 for other titles by
Barbara Cartland*

BARBARA CARTLAND

# THE RUTHLESS RAKE

A PAN ORIGINAL

PAN BOOKS LTD
LONDON AND SYDNEY

First published 1974 by Pan Books Ltd,
Cavaye Place, London SW10 9PG

ISBN 0 330 23920 1

Printed in Great Britain by
Richard Clay (The Chaucer Press), Ltd, Bungay, Suffolk

## Author's Note

The conditions at Newgate with its debauchery, foul discomfort, filth, squalor, evil and moral deterioration continued until Elizabeth Fry started her reforms in 1815.

The prison was the worst source of gaol fever, with a high mortality rate for many years. The whipping of females was not abolished until 1817.

The Prince of Wales' friends are all historical characters. The Prince was a keen supporter of boxing until the Summer of 1790, two months after the story opens, when he saw a man killed in the ring at Brighton and never again attended a fight.

# Chapter One

There was a rough ring made by a huge crowd sitting, kneeling or lying on the ground.

On one side a hastily improvised haycock, covered in rugs, made a seat for the Prince of Wales.

Outside the ring of all classes, packed and intent, there were the chariots, chaises, phaetons, gigs, waggons and carts in which the more distinguished and wealthy members of the company had arrived.

Under a clear sky on the short grass, Tom Tully, the Wiltshire giant of the ring backed by the Prince of Wales and the majority of his friends, was matched against Nat Baggot, a smaller and unknown fighter sponsored by the Earl of Rothingham.

Tom Tully, resolute of jaw, heavy-muscled and looking as indomitable as the Rock of Gibraltar seemed impervious to blows from the smaller man.

Yet Nat Baggot, quick-eyed and swift-footed, appeared unabashed by his formidable opponent.

They had been fighting for over an hour and it seemed as if neither could ever be the winner.

Then behind the crowd of vehicles there came the sound of hurrying hooves and quickly turning wheels.

A four-in-hand was hurtling across the Common at a tremendous speed, driven by a gentleman with such expertise that despite the allurement of the mill many of the crowd turned to watch his prowess.

He drew up his horse with a flourish, flung the reins to

his groom and stepped down with an athletic ease that belied his height.

His hat was set raffishly on his own dark unpowdered hair, his boots had been polished with champagne until they reflected as brightly as a mirror.

The tops were as pure white as Beau Brummel had decided was correct for Gentlemen of Fashion.

Once on the ground the Gentleman appeared not to hurry, but to walk with a bored and almost indifferent air towards the seats occupied by the Prince of Wales and his friends.

Without his requesting it the crowd made way for him to pass through as if his authority was unquestioned.

Having reached his objective, he bowed to the Prince and sat down beside him, a place having been made for him automatically by the previous occupier.

The Prince glanced at him frowning, but did not speak and almost ostentatiously turned his head again to watch the contest.

The newcomer settled himself comfortably and also appeared intent on the battle taking place in front of him.

There was an ugly cut on Nat Baggot's cheek and his nose was bleeding, yet as they struck, parried and feinted the smaller man was smiling, while it appeared as if Tom Tully was looking grimmer than usual.

Then unexpectedly there came a sudden rush of feet, the panting hiss of breath, the shock of several vicious blows from already bleeding knuckles, and Tom Tully the unbeaten champion threw up his arms, staggered back the length of the ring and went down with a crash.

For a moment there was the pregnant silence of astonishment.

Then the top-hatted seconds who had been shadowing the combatants in their sleeves, looked towards the referee. He began his slow count:

"One ... two ... three ... four..."

There were shouts and yells from the crowd.

"Come on, Tom, up wi' ye. Ye've never been a beaten yet ... eight ... nine ... ten!"

There were shouts and cat-calls, applause and a few jeers as Nat Baggot's hand was held high and the match was over.

"Curse you, Rothingham!" the Prince said to the Gentleman at his side. "I owe you three hundred guineas and you cannot even trouble to be present for the best part of the fight."

"I can only proffer my most sincere apologies, Sire," the Earl of Rothingham drawled. "My excuse is I was unexpectedly delayed by circumstances – most alluring and delectable – over which I had no control."

The Prince tried to look severe and failed.

Then his smile broadened and suddenly he was laughing and his friends were laughing with him.

"Damn it you are incorrigible!" he exclaimed. "Come, luncheon is waiting for us at Carlton House."

The Prince led the way towards his Phaeton the crowd cheering him as he passed through them. He ignored his fallen champion who had cost him so much money.

The Earl of Rothingham delayed leaving the ring to shake Nat Baggot by the hand. He gave him a purse in which a number of gold coins clinked pleasantly and promised him another fight in the near future.

Then accepting, apparently uninterested, the congratulations of both the gentlemen and the hoi-polloi he too moved towards his horses.

Luncheon at Carlton House was as usual an elaborate meal with, in the opinion of many of His Royal Highness's guests, too many courses.

The Prince appeared to enjoy them all, as he enjoyed most of the good things in life, with an eager, greedy enthusiasm.

Looking at him as he sat at the top of the table, the Earl thought that however handsome he might be he was already running to fat.

Yet His Royal Highness at twenty-seven was little more than a handsome rollicking boy with a reckless sense of humour.

Ever since he had returned to England, the Earl had found himself without making any effort, drawn closer day by day into the gay, inconsequent hard-drinking, high gambling set which surrounded the Prince of Wales.

He was a few years older and certainly more experienced than most of its members.

Yet they insisted he should take part in their youthful enthusiasms, their sporting interests and their endless pursuit of beautiful women.

The young lordlings were never more entertaining or more democratic than when they forgathered with their favourite champions at Zimmers Hotel or met each other for their lessons in the manly sport of boxing in Gentleman Jackson's Rooms in Bond Street.

The Earl after years abroad had been surprised when, soon after he arrived in England three years ago in 1787, he had seen the Jew Mendoza beat Martin in the presence of the Prince of Wales and be escorted back to London with lighted torches and a crowd singing "See the Conquering Hero Comes".

"Their boxing interests," an eminent soldier had said to the Earl on the ship which brought them both back from India, "have created a sense of fair play in England today which from the highest in the land to the lowest makes them enforce a just sportsmanship as rigidly as the Knights of the Round table enforced the laws of Chivalry."

"Tell me more about England today," the Earl suggested. "I have been abroad for a long time."

The older man had paused a moment.

"You will think I am being romantic or at least exaggerating," he said, "if I tell you that it is a golden age, and the society which moves in it is more gracious, more subtle and better balanced than anything on earth since the days of Ancient Greece."

"Can that be true?" the Earl asked.

"The nobility of England," the General replied, "lead the country because they are healthy, gregarious and generous. They govern without a police force, without a Bastille and virtually without a Civil Service. They succeed by sheer assurance and personality."

He paused and continued slowly:

"In my opinion England today could beat every other nation in the world with one hand tied behind its back."

"I am afraid not everyone would agree with you," the Earl remarked with obvious disbelief.

"You will see for yourself," the General replied.

The Prince of Wales perhaps exemplified the contrasts in the English character.

He had many talents, he was artistic, well educated from a literary point of view, extremely civilised where good behaviour, manners and cleanliness were concerned.

Yet, like the people over whom his father reigned, he enjoyed rough jokes, tolerated a certain amount of cruelty, could be ruthless, and as someone said:

"He loves horses as dearly as women, and probably there is no gentleman in England more expert in appreciation of two such beautiful creations."

It was of women that the Prince obviously wished to speak with the Earl when the luncheon was over and the rest of his guests had departed.

"If you are not leaving for a moment, Rothingham," he said, "I wish to talk with you."

He led the way as he spoke into one of the ornate and fantastically decorated salons which had cost an exorbitant amount of money – a debt as yet unpaid.

"You make me apprehensive, Sire," the Earl remarked.

The Prince flung himself down in a comfortable chair and made a gesture which invited the Earl to sit opposite him.

It seemed to the latter as if his host looked him over speculatively, almost as if the two of them were in a ring sparring for an opening.

The Prince's train of thought however was diverted by the elegance of the Earl's blue coat worn over a pair of spotless white breeches.

Plain and unornamented it was sported by its owner with a style and yet at the same time with an air of comfort which the Prince vainly sought to obtain.

"Curse it, Rothingham, who is your tailor?" he asked, "Weston never made that coat."

"No, I never cared for Weston," the Earl replied, "this came from Schultz."

"Then he can make one for me," the Prince said, "and I wish I could get my valet to tie a cravat as skilfully as yours."

"I tie my own," the Earl answered.

"You tie them yourself!" the Prince exclaimed in astonishment.

"I have done so for many years," the Earl replied. "I find I can do it quicker and in most cases far better than any valet."

"That is just what is wrong with you," the Prince said snappily, "you are too damned self-sufficient. And incidentally it is on that subject I wish to speak."

There was a suspicion of a twinkle in the Earl's half-closed eyes, as if he guessed what was coming.

His deep blue eyes were strangely arresting. They could be disturbingly penetrating and his enemies found them hard to meet.

There was usually a cynical smile on his lips as if he found, if not life, at any rate those in it secretly amusing.

There was a disconcerting directness about him, and yet at the same time anyone who knew him well felt that he had reserves that were too deep for superficial comprehension.

Lean without an ounce of spare flesh on his frame, his clear-cut features were arrestingly handsome and commanded attention and an often unwilling respect.

His long sojourn abroad had neither impaired his appearance nor had it curtailed his achievements in the world of sport.

A Corinthian in the way he tooled his horseflesh, a race-horse owner to be reckoned with, a patron of the boxing-ring, he, himself was no mean pugilist.

It was not surprising, the Prince thought looking at the Earl, that women clustered round him like bees around a honey-pot.

"Well, Sire, I am waiting," the Earl said in his deep voice. "For what misdemeanour am I to be reprimanded on this occasion?"

"Do not make me sound like a Tutor," the Prince replied. "I am speaking for your own good."

"Then it is sure to be unpleasant, Sire," the Earl drawled seating himself more comfortably in the armchair.

"Not unpleasant," the Prince replied, "but a slight embarrassment."

The Earl did not answer but merely raised his eyebrows.

"Lady Elaine Wilmot has been talking to Mrs. Fitzherbert," the Prince said at length.

The twinkle in the Earl's eyes was even more pronounced.

"Indeed, Sire! On what particular subject?"

"As if you did not know the answer," the Prince replied. "Yourself of course! And Mrs. Fitzherbert feels, and I do too, that Lady Elaine would make you a very suitable wife, Rothingham."

"In what way suitable?" the Earl asked.

The Prince considered a moment.

"She is beautiful, in fact Lady Elaine has been the Incomparable and the Toast of St. James's for several years."

"I am well aware of that," the Earl murmured.

"She is amusing, witty and – experienced."

The Prince paused a moment.

"I never could stand inexperienced women myself. All that girlish giggling and simpering are enough to depress any man!"

13

"True enough, Sire," the Earl agreed.

He remembered that Mrs. Fitzherbert was nine years older than the Prince.

Whether or not, as rumour had it, they were secretly married, they both appeared to be happy in each other's company.

There was a pause and then the Prince asked:

"Well?" It was a question.

The Earl smiled and it gave his face a raffish inconceiving look. He had the expression of an outlaw who would take what he desired by force. It was easy to see why women found him irresistible.

"I am yours to command, Sire, where my service, my sword and my fortune is concerned," he said. "But as regards marriage, I must beg your leave to choose my own bride."

The Prince shook his head.

"Mrs. Fitzherbert will be disappointed."

"And so unfortunately will Lady Elaine," the Earl added. "But, Sire, I find so many women delightful that I have no desire to shackle myself to one for the rest of my life."

"You mean you do not intend to marry?" the Prince asked.

"I intend to enjoy myself, Sire. When one has such a choice of beautiful flowers, why should one confine oneself to picking just one?"

The Prince threw back his head and laughed.

"As I have said before, Rothingham, you are incorrigible. The trouble is you are a rake."

"An unrepentant one, Sire."

"Marriage is a very competitive institution," the Prince said almost coaxingly.

"If one desires comfort," the Earl agreed. "At the same time I would find it hard not to wonder just how much of my wife's affection was engendered by the comfort of my Bank balance!"

"You cannot be so cynical!" the Prince cried.

"I have yet, Sire, to meet the woman who would contemplate marriage with me without the comfort of knowing I could house, clothe and feed her in the manner she most desires."

"And who should blame her?" the Prince asked almost aggressively. "Being without money is a cursed embarrassment, as I know to my cost! But you are a dashing figure of a man, Rothingham! There must be any number of fair charmers who would love you for yourself alone."

"We were talking of marriage, Sire," the Earl said. "Love is a very different kettle of fish."

"Very well, continue to be a rake and a roué!" the Prince exclaimed crossly.

Then with one of his flashes of intuition which his friends knew well he added:

"No, that is not true. You are not a roué. You are too autocratic, too inflexible, too . . ."

The Prince hesitated for words.

"Would ruthless be the word you require, Sire?" the Earl suggested.

"Yes it is," the Prince agreed. "You are ruthless, Rothingham, in many ways. Look how you turned that fellow Mainwaring out of his Clubs and made everyone ostracise him."

"He deserved it, Sire," the Earl replied.

"May be, but few other men would have had the determination to punish him in such a way."

The Prince paused.

"Yes, ruthless is the right description for you, Rothingham, but perhaps a wife would be able to change that."

"I doubt it, Sire."

"All the same," the Prince continued, "you will need an heir, if your fortune is as large as it is reported to be."

There was an obvious curiosity in His Royal Highness's expression and the Earl replied:

"For once such reports are true. I am, as it happens, extremely warm in the pocket."

"I am full of curiosity as to how you achieved it," the Prince said. "After all, if I am not mistaken, you left England when you were twenty-one without a penny piece to your name."

"My father was bankrupt," the Earl replied, and his voice was hard. "He had gambled away every penny of the family fortune and, as if that was not enough, created a scandal by getting himself killed in a duel in discreditable circumstances."

"It was all very regrettable," the Prince said. "I remember the King speaking of it with deep concern."

"I was fortunate enough," the Earl continued, "to transfer into a regiment that was going to India. It cannot be of particular interest to your Royal Highness, but the wound I received, which was a minor one in a very minor battle, changed my whole life."

"How?" the Prince asked.

There was no doubt of his interest and the Earl went on :

"I was invalided out of the Army. Having no money with which to return to England, I looked about me for some sort of occupation which might be remunerative. The aristocrats of England might find it reprehensible, but I went into trade."

"Trade?" the Prince questioned.

"I was extremely fortunate," the Earl said, "and I was helped by a very alluring pair of dark eyes in getting to know the Merchants who are making enormous fortunes in this oriental El Dorado of which in the next few years we will hear a great deal more."

"Tell me about it," the Prince demanded with a most flattering expression of curiosity.

"Your Royal Highness is well aware that England is receiving from India an ever-growing stream of spices, indigo, sugar, ivory, ebony, tea, sandalwood, salt-petre and silks. It is this trade and the ships which carry it, in which I managed to get a share, which has enabled me not only to reinstate myself, but to retrieve my father's reputation."

"Mrs. Fitzherbert tells me you paid back all his debts," the Prince said.

"Every farthing," the Earl answered, "and with interest! If I may say so, the slate is clear."

"And your estates?"

"Those too I have recovered but only in the past few weeks," the Earl said. "Twenty-three years ago, when my father began to lose his possessions one by one in reckless gaming, a cousin, Colonel Fitzroy Roth, came forward and took over the family house and the great acreage surrounding it. He assumed all liability for our tenants and pensioners, the herd and other commitments, on condition that it remained his for his lifetime."

"You mean he has now died?" the Prince asked.

"A few weeks ago," the Earl replied, "and so I have now come into my own."

There was a faint note of elation in his voice.

"I am glad for your sake, Rothingham, but at the same time all the more you will now need a wife to grace the head of your table."

"There are, I assure you, Sire, many applicants for the position," the Earl replied.

"That I can quite believe!" the Prince ejaculated. "But you are still determined not to marry?"

"I intend to enjoy myself for many years as yet," the Earl declared. "Perhaps when I am in my dotage I may find some comfortable creature to toady to my idiosyncrasies and cosset my failing health. Until then..."

The Earl paused.

"Until then, you will 'play the field'?" the Prince suggested.

"Exactly! Your Royal Highness could not have expressed it better."

"Well, Lady Elaine will have a long wait," the Prince said rising to his feet.

"She will indeed," the Earl agreed, "but doubtless she will

speedily find an alternative attraction with which to console herself."

"You underestimate the fidelity of a woman's heart," the Prince said, "or the damage you may inflict on it."

"I have always found," the Earl said, "that diamonds have an exceptionally restorative quality. I have never yet met a woman who could refuse such medicine."

The Prince laughed and said:

"Will you come with me to Newmarket tomorrow?"

"I regret, Sire, I must decline such a delightful invitation, but I have already arranged to visit my Estate. It is almost a lifetime since I saw 'King's Keep' and I am sure there are many alterations and improvements to be put in hand. But I shall not be away for more than two or three days."

"Then I shall eagerly await your return," the Prince said. "I find, Rothingham, the dullest party is amusing when you are present."

"I thank you, Sire, but let us avoid dull parties at all cost. There is at the end of the week to be a very amusing evening with the Corps de Ballet from the Opera. It would be deeply appreciated if you could find your way to be present."

"The Corps de Ballet, eh?" The Prince asked. "I do not mind telling you, Rothingham, I find some of them extremely good-looking."

"They are indeed an enchanting collection," the Earl said. "May I therefore count on your presence next Thursday at 11 o'clock?"

"You may indeed," the Prince replied. "Are you giving the party?"

"I imagine I will be presented with the bill," the Earl replied.

"And who could better afford it?" the Prince exclaimed. "And that reminds me, Rothingham, I hear you paid two thousand guineas for those greys you were driving yesterday. Finest pair of horseflesh I have seen for some time! I wanted them myself when they came up at Tattersalls, but they were beyond my touch."

"You saw them?" the Earl enquired.

"I saw them and admired them," the Prince replied, "and Mrs. Fitzherbert agreed with me that they were the most exceptional cattle on which we had either of us set eyes for a long time."

"Well, if Mrs. Fitzherbert liked them," the Earl said slowly, "allow me, Sire, to make her a present of them. I would not wish her to be disappointed."

The Prince's face lit up.

"Do you mean that, Rothingham? By Jove, you are a generous chap! But I ought not to accept such a gift, as you well know."

"If we either of us did only the things we should do, Your Royal Highness, the world would be a very dreary place."

The Prince laughed and put his hand on his friend's shoulder.

"Then if you mean what you say, I accept with thanks. It is generous of you, damned generous, and I shall not forget it."

"They shall be delivered to your stable tomorrow," the Earl said, "and I will rely on you, Sire, to see that they make my peace with Mrs. Fitzherbert. Perhaps she would be gracious enough to soothe the injured feelings of Lady Elaine."

The Prince laughed.

"I might have known there was some condition attached to such generosity!"

"You cannot expect me to forget so quickly the trader's instinct," the Earl retorted.

The Prince was laughing as they went from the Salon into the broad corridor which led towards the stairs. But the Earl's lazy blue eyes showed cynical amusement.

On leaving Carlton House the Earl found waiting for him his yellow and black High-Perched Phaeton in which he drove to a house in Curzon Street.

The door was opened by a manservant whom His Lordship greeted familiarly.

"Good afternoon, John. Is Her Ladyship in?"

"Yes, M'Lord. Her Ladyship is upstairs trying on gowns with Madame Bertin."

"It sounds expensive," the Earl remarked. "I will find my own way up."

He walked quickly up the staircase and crossing the landing knocked perfunctorily on a door and entered before there could be an answer.

In the centre of a bed-room which was decorated in rose-pink silk, Lady Elaine Wilmot, wearing a diaphanous négligée of lime-coloured gauze, was inspecting a gown held out to her by Madame Bertin, the most exclusive dress-maker in Bond Street.

Madame had been lady's-maid to Marie Antoinette.

But when the first rumblings of revolution had started in France, she had quickly crossed the Channel and established herself as an arbiter of fashion to the Beau Monde.

The gown Lady Elaine was inspecting was full-skirted, her tightly laced waist was encircled by a sash and the low décolletage was veiled by a fine muslin fichu in the fashion set by the Queen of France and which had been adopted by most English ladies of Quality.

As the door opened, Lady Elaine turned her head indifferently as if she expected the entrance of a servant.

When she saw the Earl she gave a cry of delight.

"Ancelin, I was not expecting you!"

She ran towards him, oblivious of the fact that silhouetted against the light from the window her transparent négligée revealed the exquisite perfection of her naked body.

The Earl took the two hands which she held out to him and raised them to his lips.

"Can it be possible that you are in need of more fripperies?" he demanded.

Lady Elaine pouted at him prettily, but her eyes pleaded as she said:

"I have nothing to wear and you did say . . ."

"Yes, I did say," the Earl replied good-humouredly.

Lady Elaine gave a quick sigh of relief and turned to Madame Bertin.

"Let me have the four gowns we have chosen as quickly as possible," she said.

"*Certainement*, M'Lady. *Et le compte* to his Lordship as usual?"

"As usual," the Earl agreed before Lady Elaine could speak.

Madame Bertin and an assistant who had remained discreetly in the corner of the room collected their boxes, their gowns, several rolls of silk and curtseyed themselves out of the bed-room.

As soon as the door closed behind them, Lady Elaine moved nearer to the Earl and put her arms round his neck.

"You are so kind to me," she said. "I was half afraid you would think me extravagant in buying new gowns when you have only recently paid the old harridan's exorbitant bill."

"Think you extravagant?" the Earl asked mockingly. "What could have put such an idea into your pretty little head?"

He looked down at her as he spoke, seeing the slanting dark fringed eyes, the winged eyebrows which matched the raven curls elegantly arranged to frame the oval perfection of her face.

There was no doubt that Lady Elaine was a great beauty.

The whiteness of her skin, the seductiveness of her large eyes and her full sensuous mouth had been acclaimed by almost every Buck in London.

Daughter of a Duke, she had however made a disastrous marriage almost before she had left the School-room. It was however, fortunately of short duration.

Her husband, wild, improvident and a heavy drinker, had been killed in a crazy midnight Steeple-chase across country when most of the riders were too foxed to know where they were going or to keep astride their horses.

It was as a dazzling, beautiful and extremely ambitious widow that Lady Elaine had startled the *Beau Monde*.

There were many people who disapproved of her.

The older most staid hostesses, who clustered around the Court at Buckingham House and were scandalised by the impropriety of the Prince of Wales, did their best to cold-shoulder Lady Elaine, but without avail.

It was obvious she would become an intimate of the Carlton House Set and also with such ancestry, few of the aristocracy could actually close their doors to her if she demanded entry.

Lady Elaine swept through social London like a lighted torch.

It was obvious when the Earl of Rothingham appeared and speedily achieved for himself a reputation of rakishness and extravagance, that their names should be coupled and they should inevitably be drawn to each other as if by magnetism.

"Did you attend the mill this morning?" Lady Elaine asked.

"I did," the Earl replied, "and my man won."

"That must have infuriated the Prince!"

"His Royal Highness bet heavily on Tom Tully. He was certain his choice must be the victor. But he has forgiven me."

"Did you have luncheon at Carlton House?"

There was something in the way Lady Elaine asked the question that told the Earl she was well aware that the Prince would choose such an opportunity to speak to him about their relationship.

"Yes I had luncheon at Carlton House," the Earl replied slowly.

"And were you alone with the Prince at any moment?"

"We had quite a long talk after the other guests had departed."

He waited sensing her anxiety. There was something cruel about the twist of his lips.

"Did the Prince mention ... me?" Lady Elaine asked hesitantly.

"He spoke of you like a father," the Earl replied, "or, should I say, like a matrimonial match-maker?"

There was a pause.

"And what was your answer?" Lady Elaine whispered.

She raised her face as she spoke so that her red lips slightly parted were very inviting and very near to the Earl's.

"I assured the Prince," the Earl said, putting his arms round her and feeling the warmth of her body as she drew nearer to him, "that while I loved beautiful women – I loved my freedom more."

"How could you!"

There was no mistaking the sudden sharp note in Lady Elaine's voice. In answer the Earl drew her closer.

"Must you be so greedy?"

"What do you mean greedy?" she asked.

"I am ready to offer you so much! So much that will amuse and gratify us both," he replied. "But not, my dear, a wedding-ring. That is too expensive even for me to afford."

Lady Elaine's arms went round the Earl's neck and she drew his face down to hers.

"But I love you," she whispered, "I love you."

In answer the Earl crushed his lips against hers.

He felt a burning desire rise within them both, tempestuous, fiery and compelling, and he picked her up in his arms.

She felt him carry her towards the bed, she took her lips from his and threw back her head.

"You want me and – I want you," she said her voice deep with passion, "oh, why – why will you not marry me?"

"You are too attractive to be shackled to only one man," the Earl answered and she knew he mocked her.

She gave a cry of protest but she had no chance to say more.

He tumbled her down on the bed against the pillows and

then his mouth, hard passionate and demanding, was on hers and all argument was forgotten.

It was some time later that the Earl drove his horses from Curzon Street into Berkeley Square and turned them towards Piccadilly.

At Covent Garden Opera House a rehearsal was in progress.

Entering by the stage door, the Earl made his way up the twisting iron staircase to a small dressing-room. Michelle Latour had risen from the rank and file of the Corps de Ballet to a small part. She was therefore entitled to a dressing-room.

The room filled with baskets, bouquets and vases of flowers was empty.

The Earl waited for nearly five minutes before there was the clatter of feet on the stairs and Michelle came running into the room.

At the sight of the Earl she flung out her arms and ran gracefully like a bird in flight to lay her head against his shoulder.

"*Mon cher*, why you not tell me you come?" she asked, a broken accent giving a piquancy and an attraction to her words.

"I was not sure what time I would be here," the Earl replied, "but I came to tell you, Michelle, that I am leaving for the country immediately."

"Tonight?"

"Yes."

"*Tiens!* Then we cannot 'ave ze supper together. *C'est triste* – it is sad – very sad for me."

"I shall not be away long," the Earl said.

"I miss you, I miss you! Oh so very much!" Michelle murmured. "I shall, how you say – add up ze hours 'til you return."

"I shall be in London for our party on Thursday," the Earl said. "The Prince of Wales has promised to be present."

"The Prince of Wales, *c'est merveilleux*! It will make everyone 'appy."

"It means so much to you?" the Earl enquired.

Michelle shrugged her white shoulders.

"*Pas du tout!* All that matters to me is that you should be there."

"You say that very prettily," the Earl said, "but I fear, Michelle, like all your sex, you are a snob! An Earl is perhaps two feathers in your cap, but the Prince of Wales is a whole fantail of them."

Michelle laughed and extricated herself from his arms.

"You look *très chic*, verry dashing, *Mon Cher*. It is true that you go to ze country alone?"

"I assure you I travel alone," the Earl answered.

"And when you arrive, when you see again *ce Château* where you lived as a child, you will 'ave guests. *Une jolie femme, n'est ce pas?*"

"No pretty ladies," the Earl replied. "I shall see factors and farm managers, woodmen and carpenters. I shall be talking of improvements and renovations but not of love."

"*Voila!* I will not be jealous," Michelle said, "but I shall be lonely in that *charmante petite résidence* you 'ave given me. It is a dear little house and I love it verry much, *mais* without you it is empty!"

"I am flattered," the Earl replied. "It is always a pleasure to give you presents, Michelle, and when I return we must look for that bracelet I promised you. One that will match the ear-rings that glitter so entrancingly in your little ears."

"You will give me ze diamond bracelet I 'ave seen in Bond Street, *oui?*"

"We will talk about it on Thursday," the Earl promised, "and now I must go. Behave yourself while I am away."

He put his fingers under her chin and turned her face up to his.

"I have an aversion to anyone keeping my bed warm when I am not in it."

"Do you think I could take another lover when you 'ave been so kind, so verry kind and generous to me?" Michelle asked. "*Hélas!* 'Ow could you think such a thing of me? 'Ow can you imagine I am such a low creature?"

"I think you protest very eloquently," the Earl said with a sarcastic note in his voice. "And I should suggest to your friend that the next time he visits you he should be careful not to leave his gloves behind. Such forgetfulness is so easily misconstrued."

He glanced as he spoke towards the side of the dressing-table on which reposed a pair of kid gloves obviously of a masculine size and shape.

Michelle gave a little scream of anger.

"*Cet homme est fou!*" she said, and then quickly, as if to cover her lapse. "*Non, non,* they belong to no friend of mine! My dresser found them in ze corridor. Some gentleman must have dropped them when visiting one of ze girls."

The Earl smiled and it was insulting.

"You lie most fluently and almost convincingly," he said, and before she could reply he had gone from the dressing-room leaving Michelle staring after him uncertainly.

She listened to his footsteps receding into the distance and then she stamped her foot.

"*Quel imbécile! Salaud!*" she exclaimed over and over again.

She went towards the mirror over the dressing-table, her eyes blazing, and she took up the gloves, then threw them on the floor and stamped on them.

The Earl was still smiling, although there was no humour in it, as he swung himself up on the seat of his High-Perched Phaeton and took up the reins from his groom.

There was a hard ruthless look in his eyes.

He had no illusions about the morals of the 'little bits of muslin' he took under his protection, but at the same time he disliked being lied to and deceived.

He had not really imagined that Michelle was deceiving

26

him, it had been a bow drawn at a venture. But her reaction had told him the truth.

It annoyed him because he knew it was only greed for money and more money which made her share her favours.

The Earl had a good idea who Michelle's paramour might be.

He was aware that a wealthy cit had been interested in her long before he had appeared on the scene. She had made fun of her middle-aged vulgar admirer. But he was rich and generous!

Michelle could not resist taking and taking...

The Earl made a decision. He was no longer interested in Michelle. He would send her the usual farewell gift and his secretary would see that she vacated the home in which he had installed her, as speedily as possible.

There was a red-haired dancer in the chorus who had a vivacious vitality which attracted him. He decided to make her acquaintance on his return to London.

Michelle was dismissed from his Lordship's thoughts as if she had never existed.

The narrow streets through which the Earl drove his horses with great expertise were thronged with coaches and drays.

Women in ragged shawls and straw bonnets, pock-marked beggars, shifty-eyed pick-pockets, and tightly-stocked young men with tall fluffy beaver hats cluttered the dirty pavements.

The Earl reached the fashionable roads and squares of Mayfair.

Here a wealth of servants with cockaded hats sat red-nosed on the draped boxes of coaches bearing their masters' coat-of-arms, or stood erect with tall silver-topped canes on their swinging platforms.

The bedizened flunkeys invariably had a following of noisy bare-footed urchins, who half-jeeringly, half-admiringly pursued them wherever they went.

Running beside a vehicle or swinging themselves on behind, they would risk the lash of the whip with an impudent gesture and a bawdy word of derision.

On reaching Rothingham House the Earl stepped down from the Phaeton and passing though a line of bowing servants found his Butler waiting for him in the hall.

"Bring me wine to the Library, Meadstone," he said, "and order the four-in-hand with fresh horses. I shall leave in half an hour."

"The luggage in the charge of Your Lordship's valets has already gone ahead, M'Lord."

"Good!" the Earl exclaimed as he walked across the hall.

He entered the Library, a long room over-looking a small flower filled garden at the back of the house.

A flunkey brought a decanter of wine on a silver salver and set it down on a small table.

Meadstone poured out a glass and handed it to the Earl.

He sipped it slowly before he said:

"I noticed last night that one of the footmen, Henry I think, was badly powdered and his stockings were wrinkled."

"I regret, M'Lord, that I did not notice Henry's appearance until he was already in the Dining-room," Meadstone apologised.

"Why?"

"Why did I not notice him, M'Lord?" Meadstone hesitated before he continued. "Henry was a trifle late on duty, M'Lord."

"Dismiss him!"

"Dismiss, M'Lord?"

There was a note of dismay in the Butler's voice.

"Immediately! I pay for perfection – I expect it!"

"But, M'Lord—"

"I said immediately."

"Yes, M'Lord."

There was silence while Meadstone refilled the Earl's glass. Then with an effort he said respectfully:

"I hope Your Lordship will find everything in good order

at 'King's Keep'. It will be like old times to know it is back in Your Lordship's hands."

"It must have altered a great deal since I was there," the Earl said. "Do you realise, Meadstone, I was nine when I left the country, twenty three years ago."

"I remember it well, M'Lord. Your father, his late Lordship was in straitened circumstances that year."

"He was always in straitened circumstances," the Earl observed and his voice was harsh.

"Indeed, M'Lord, things were very difficult – very difficult indeed."

"Did you ever get paid all you were owed?" the Earl asked.

"Not until you reimbursed me, M'Lord, on your return from abroad."

"Why did you not leave and find other employment?" the Earl asked. "There must have been six or seven of you here struggling on year after year, my father living on what he could sell. The mirrors, the furniture, the pictures, never paying his debts except with promises. Why did you stay?"

Meadstone looked embarrassed.

"I think Your Lordship knows the answer," he said at length. "We belonged, as one might say. My father and his father before him had served the Roth family. It'd not have been right for us to have left when things were hard."

"Hard!" the Earl ejaculated. "Unpaid, half starved!"

He paused and looked at the butler.

"Yes, I do understand," he said gently, "and all I can say, Meadstone, is thank you – thank you all. We have come through the hard times, now I will see there are no more of them."

"You suffered too, Master Ancelin," Meadstone said, relapsing his formality and addressing the Earl in the manner he had done when he was a child.

"We will not talk of that!" the Earl said sharply. "Come,

29

Meadstone, I must change before I set out for the country. Is there anyone to attend to me?"

"I will do so myself, M'Lord, and there is a young footman I am training, if you will permit him to watch."

"I am sure he will find it most instructive," the Earl answered.

He drained his glass and turned towards the stairs.

"To tell the truth, Meadstone," he said, "I feel quite apprehensive at the thought of seeing King's Keep again. One should never walk back into the past. There is always a chance one will be bitterly disappointed."

"Not with King's Keep, M'Lord," Meadstone said. "It has survived for 300 years. I don't think Your Lordship'll be disappointed."

"I would not bet on it," the Earl replied, but he was not sneering.

# Chapter Two

The Earl awoke early and lay for a while in the huge four-poster bed in which generations of Roths had been born and died, thinking of his home.

He then rose and crossing the room pulled back the curtains over the mullion windows and looked out into the April sunshine.

He thought, as he had done last night when he arrived at King's Keep just as the sun was setting, that there was no more beautiful place in the whole world.

Wisps of morning mist still lay over the two silver lakes linked by a bridge which carried the drive into the park. Under the great oak trees a carpet of daffodils was a golden herald of Spring.

There were daffodils too sloping down to the lakes to join the kingcups and the wild iris which were just coming into flower, and there were daffodils impudently peeping between the shrubs which bordered the green lawns.

"Velvet not grass," as one Royal admirer had once said of them.

King's Keep had originally been a Monastery, but after it had been looted and left half-ruined by Henry VIII, the land had reverted to the Crown.

Sir Thomas Roth, a courtier to Queen Elizabeth I, had purchased all that was left of the Monastery and erected a great house worthy of his position at Court and a monument to his huge fortune.

In this building he had kept two of the inner courts which rested upon the foundation of the monastic cloister, but there was nothing medieval about the house itself and King's Keep became one of the most breathtakingly beautiful buildings in the whole country.

It was situated almost in a hollow between two hills covered with woods.

"A diamond in a green setting," someone had said of it poetically, and one of the many Kings who had stayed there had commented enviously :

"It is too good for a subject !"

The house had changed its name when Charles II as a young Prince had hidden in one of its secret chambers for three nights from the Cromwellian troops. On leaving he had said to Sir John Roth :

"When I become King this house shall be renamed 'King's Keep', for it has indeed kept me safe."

Sir John was dead when the restoration came, but his son became the first Earl of Rothingham and King's Keep was a favourite place for the King and his roistering courtiers to take their lady loves.

The first Earl was not a particularly good poet, but eloquent and he carved over a bedroom door :

> "King's Keep,
>     Where morals sleep
>     And lovers meet."

It must have been the first Earl who had brought a new raffish strain into the Roth blood.

The portraits of the previous owners of King's Keep were of good-looking staid men with an air of serious concentration about them, but the first Earl distinctly resembled his present successor.

All down the succeeding centuries there had been Rothinghams looking like handsome buccaneers who had sailed round the world in search of adventure, leaving behind them legends of their conquests of the fair sex and of their phenomenal good fortune as gamesters.

It was unfortunate, the Earl thought dryly, that his father had been the exception where 'the luck of the Roths' was concerned.

He had been a gamester but an unfortunate one. While he was still quite young he gambled away a large amount of the family fortune.

He had however the attraction that all the Roths possessed for women and his wife was not only beautiful and well-born, but had also brought him a large dowry.

He contrived to run through that in a few years and when she died bearing her second child, his wild extravagances brought him to the verge of bankruptcy.

King's Keep, as the Earl had related to the Prince, was only saved by a cousin, Colonel Fitzroy Roth, who took it over at the earnest plea of his relatives, who feared to see a whole page of English history disappear on the green baize of the gaming tables of St. James's.

The Colonel saved the Estate, the house and its contents from the hands of the usurers.

The Earl, walking through the Great State Rooms thought how easily the beauty of King's Keep might have been lost forever like the priceless treasures which had filled Rothingham House in Berkeley Square.

It still hurt him even now to think of what his father had thrown away.

Roth Square in Bloomsbury, Roth Avenue in Islington, Roth Street off Piccadilly, they had all been dissipated in nights of wild gaming or sold for ridiculous sums so that more guineas could be lost on absurd and eccentric wagers at which his father never had a chance of being the winner.

He had died still challenging the fates.

"I wager you two monkeys that I live until after midnight."

It was a bet which fortunately was not accepted.

His luck had not changed and he died at two minutes to midnight in a room in which he had even sold the carpet off the floor.

Last night, after he had finished dinner, the Earl had walked through the house and thanked God that one of his relations had possessed enough pride in the family to keep some of its possessions intact.

He had moved through the Salons with their fine carvings, their pictures by Van Dyck, Lely, Rembrandt and Poussin, their inlaid furniture and unique collection of porcelain. He had looked at the great Banqueting Hall with its painted walls and magnificent ceiling which was considered to be Verrio's masterpiece.

He had even visited the State bedrooms with their huge four-poster beds, Vanderbank tapestries and French commodes brought to England at the beginning of the century by his grandfather.

It was the Fifth Earl to whom the house owed its greatest glory.

There was little he could do to improve the exterior with its magnificent ornamented stone work on the roof, its urns, its statues and its pointed towers which silhouetted against the sky, gave King's Keep a strange, almost fairylike silhouette.

When he had returned from a grand tour of Europe, he had brought back with him Italian artists, plasterers and gilders who had painted and gilded the ceilings and added some magnificent marble chimney pieces to the elegant Salons.

If the Earl had been afraid that he might be disappointed in King's Keep not having seen it since the age of nine, his fears were ungrounded.

It had always seemed to him grand and impressive and yet a place in which he belonged.

To see it again was to remember how much it had been in his thoughts during his exile from England after his father's death.

In the sweltering heat of the Indian plains, he would find himself remembering the soft drip of water from the fountains with their stone cupids, or the rustle of the leaves

34

in the shrubberies where he had sat as a small boy watching the little red squirrels running up the trees to hide their nuts.

Sometimes he would dream that he was playing hide-and-seek amongst the secret staircases, the priestholes, the great chimney-breasts and that he was pursued by those who would do him an injury, but from whom he knew he was safe so long as he remained within King's Keep.

"Mine! Mine! Mine!" he said to himself after dinner.

He walked across the lawn towards the lake and then turned to look back.

The house glowed like a great jewel against the darkness, the stars shone overhead, the lights from innumerable windows were golden and glowing.

"Mine!" he said again with a note of elation in his voice, "and I will never let you go."

He knew now it was for King's Keep he had worked so hard those long years in India.

He told himself at the time it was because he would never face again the humiliation of being poor and knowing so many things were unobtainable because he could not pay for them.

He wanted money because he loathed feeling debased in knowing the name Rothingham was synonymous with debts, broken promises, duns hammering on the door and the threat of the Fleet Prison.

That, he told himself, was something he would never endure again, but he knew now there was a great deal more to his overwhelming ambition to make money and to the determination in himself which would not let him rest.

It was because always at the back of his mind there was King's Keep for him to inherit where he could live – if he could afford it.

He thought of the long hours he had spent learning the art of buying and selling and of the people he had to associate with.

How he had been forced to ingratiate himself with those who had neither breeding or honesty, and how by sheer tact and diplomacy he had persuaded them to count him in as a partner.

The Dandies, the Bucks and the Noblemen who surrounded the Prince of Wales, the Earl thought, would be surprised if they knew to what depths he had stooped in his determination to make a fortune and how ruthless he had been.

But he, at least, had the luck of the Roths!

The impossible had become possible: in the most desperate gambles he had proved a winner, and then almost like a tidal wave he had found himself swept from financial success to financial success.

As he looked at King's Keep he had the absurd feeling that he wanted to put his arms round it and hold it close.

It was more lovely than the face of any woman he had ever seen, more perfect in its symmetry than any female body, and more comforting in its solidity than anything else in his life.

'This is what I have always wanted,' he thought.

He wondered why something cynical within himself laughed at his own enthusiasm.

'Would you be content to rusticate here as your grandfather did?' his heart asked.

He thought of how his grandfather had embellished King's Keep as another man might have embellished the woman he loved with jewels and gowns.

As he remembered the 5th Earl, he raised his eyes to where, on top of one of the hills sloping upwards towards the sky behind the house, he saw the dome of an Observatory.

It was from there his grandfather had studied the stars, finding them far more interesting than people, far more enthralling than Society.

"Now I have King's Keep," the Earl asked himself, "what else?"

He walked back to the house and much later had gone to bed full of plans for tomorrow.

He would see his Estate Agent, his Farm Manager, he would inspect the stables, he was certain there, if nowhere else, he would wish to make improvements.

His cousin would have kept only a small number of horses, his grandfather had not been a racing man.

The Earl was determined that his success on the turf these last three years should be but a beginning of his association with "the sport of Kings".

Tomorrow he would talk about engaging more trainers and grooms. He already had an idea of buying new bloodstock and breeding from his own mares.

He had fallen asleep with a hundred different ideas in his mind, and now this morning, looking out over the lake, he asked himself why he was in such a hurry.

King's Keep had retained its identity through many centuries, and now he wanted the peace of it to bring him a sense of security, something he had never felt since he was a child.

He rang for his valet and was downstairs for breakfast so early that the servants looked at him in surprise.

They had been well trained as the Earl had noticed last night with approval.

The food was well cooked although lacking perhaps the subtlety of the Chef he employed in London who was noted as one of the best in the *Beau Monde*.

Nevertheless every dish, and there was a large number of them, was delicious enough to tempt his appetite.

The silver was magnificent and the three footmen on duty were bright-faced country lads all over six foot and appeared to be proficient in their duties.

"I shall be giving house-parties, Barnham," he said to the Butler as he seated himself at the breakfast table. "The staff must be increased. I imagine the Colonel did not require a Groom of the Chambers or a Major-Domo?"

"No, M'Lord, I managed the household, Your Lordship might say, for the late Master."

"Well for the moment continue to do so," the Earl re-

37

plied, "but we shall require more footmen and doubtless the Housekeeper will want to engage new housemaids."

"It'll be nice to see the house full again, M'Lord," the Butler said.

The Earl looked at him in surprise.

"You were not here in my father's time?"

"No, M'Lord, I was a pantry boy when your Lordship's grandfather was alive. I left King's Keep to go as footman to the Duke of Norfolk and I returned fourteen years ago to take up my present position."

"You come from this part of the world?"

"I was born on the Estate, M'Lord."

"I am glad about that," the Earl said. "I am anxious to have my own people around me, people who have known King's Keep all their lives. Where possible, engage local men and women for the house."

"I'll do that, M'Lord."

The Earl sauntered through the Great Hall, with its magnificent carved staircase and marble statues, to the front door.

Outside a horse was waiting for him – an enormous black stallion, an expensive piece of horseflesh which the Earl had purchased a year ago and which he had sent to King's Keep the previous week.

He had fancied more than anything else he would want to ride over the Estate, and he did not anticipate that anything in the Colonel's stables would be spirited enough.

There was no doubt that Thunderer was in need not only of exercise, but someone on his back who could master him.

The Earl felt a sudden elation as finally after a tussle between man and horse, he got the stallion under control and they set off across the park at a gallop.

The air was mild and there was a sweet fragrance of Spring in the wind blowing against his face.

He saw the green buds on the trees and bushes, and everywhere he looked it seemed to him there was a profusion of daffodils.

He felt as if they were trumpeting his elation and his sense of triumph.

He had ridden for nearly two hours before he remembered there would be people waiting for him at the house.

He had so much to hear, so much to learn from his employees and yet nothing seemed more important than to acquaint himself with the lands of his fathers, with the woods that had stood sentinel on them for hundreds of years.

He had ridden further than he had intended and now he turned for home taking a different route, moving through the woods on the South side of the Estate and trying to find familiar landmarks.

He knew however that after the long years he had been away it would be difficult for him to remember much beyond the boundaries of the flower gardens surrounding the great house.

He found himself riding through pine trees.

Their russet red trunks grew close together and excluded most of the sunshine. Beneath them the ground was sandy and the stallion's hooves made little sound.

Suddenly he thought he heard a cry and reined in Thunderer to stand for a moment listening.

Could it be an animal, the Earl wondered, caught by a stoat or a weasel, or was it a bird protesting at his intrusion in a woodland sanctuary seldom entered by outsiders?

His cousin had not been a shooting-man and the Earl had already realised there were too few keepers on the Estate.

He had noticed a number of jays, their wings flashing vividly blue against the dark branches of the pines.

He had seen numerous black and white magpies and several carrion crows which he told himself a good keeper would have destroyed long ago.

Then as he sat listening to the soft movement of the wood around him, the whisper of the breeze, the swift shuffle of a rabbit, the squeak of a field-mouse, the coo of the wood-pigeon, he heard the sound of someone crying.

Wondering in surprise where the sound could come from, he heard nearer than he had suspected, a voice say:

"Oh darling ... how shall I live without ... you? How can I go on wondering what has ... happened to ... you? Where you have ... gone? How you are being ... treated?"

There was so much misery in the voice that the Earl was almost startled.

Then with a faint smile on his lips he thought he must be overhearing two lovers who were apparently saying good-bye to each other.

"How can I ... sleep at nights," the young voice went on, "thinking of you, knowing you are ... missing me ... knowing you will not ... understand why we are not ... together?"

The voice broke on the words and the speaker was crying again in a heart-broken manner, until with her voice thick with tears she continued:

"Supposing they are ... cruel to you ... supposing they do not understand how gentle you are ... how clever and obedient. Oh, darling ... darling ... what can I do? How can I let you go? Oh how I wish I were dead!"

The words seemed to be spoken in an agony, and then there was only the bitterness of tears and sobs which seemed almost uncontrollable.

The Earl slipped from his horse's back.

Tying the reins to the bough of a fallen tree he walked quietly towards the sound of the tears.

Only a few steps brought him through the trees to a clearing and he saw to his surprise standing immediately in front of him a magnificent horse.

The animal was cropping the young grass at its feet. It carried a lady's saddle with a pommel.

With her back to the Earl there was a woman.

She was sitting on a fallen tree trunk beside the horse and her head hidden by her hands was bowed onto her knees.

She wore a dress of pale green and the Earl could see from the slenderness of her figure that she was very young.

Her hair was swept back from her forehead and not arranged in a fashionable manner, but it appeared to curl naturally over her small head and he could not for the moment determine what colour it was.

He stood looking at her and knew that deafened by her own sobs, she had not heard him approach.

"What can I do ... how can I lose you?" she murmured.

"Surely there must be an answer to that question," the Earl said quietly. "Could we not try to find one?"

She stiffened at the sound of his voice but she did not raise her head from her hands.

After a moment as the Earl waited she replied:

"There is ... nothing you can ... do. Please ... go away."

"How do you know I cannot help you?" the Earl asked.

"No-one can ... help me," she answered.

Her voice was muffled by her hands which still covered her face.

"How can you be so sure?" the Earl enquired. "When things seem at their worst, it is then that one finds an explanation or has an idea which can change everything."

"Nothing ... can save ... Mercury," she answered, "so there is no ... point in ... talking about ... it."

The Earl sat down on another tree trunk.

He looked very elegant in his white breeches and his cutaway coat, his top hat at an angle on his dark hair. The girl was no longer sobbing but she did not raise her head.

"Why is your horse being sent away?" the Earl asked. "I am not just curious, I want to help you."

"I have told you ... no-one can ... help," she replied.

Her voice helpless, almost childlike, while her breath was still coming fitfully between her lips from the violence of her tears.

"Why not?" the Earl enquired.

"He is to be ... sold on ... Saturday," she answered. "I do not mind about the ... other things ... the house ... the furniture but ... Mercury will not ... understand."

"No, he will not understand," the Earl agreed reflectively.

41

"He has been with ... me ever since he was a ... foal,"
the girl said. "I have looked after him ... I have fed him and
groomed him. He has never even been... ridden by ...
anyone else. Supposing ... supposing someone was ... cruel
to him?"

Again there was an agony in the young voice which was
strangely moving.

"I cannot believe anyone would be cruel to such a fine
animal," the Earl said.

The girl raised her face a little to look at her horse. The
Earl had a glimpse of a small straight nose and lips which
trembled.

Then she turned her head aside as if she did not wish him
to look at her face.

"There is ... nothing you can ... do," she replied. "Please
go away. You are trespassing."

"Do these woods belong to you?" the Earl enquired.

"No, but I am allowed to ride in them," the girl answered, "and you will not have had permission. So please
go back to the village, you will find it a little way down
there to the left."

She pointed with her hand as she spoke.

"The village of Whitley?" the Earl asked.

"That is right. You must have lost your way."

"I would still like to help you," he said.

"I have told you," she replied almost angrily, "Mercury
has to be sold, it is in part a debt of ... honour. Gaming
debts are, you know! And there are other ... amounts that
must be paid or else ..."

Her voice died away.

"Or else..." the Earl prompted.

"My father will go to ... prison!"

She almost whispered the words as if she spoke to herself.

"And what will happen to you?" the Earl asked tentatively. "When your house is sold, and Mercury is gone,
where will you go?"

"I have no idea," the girl answered, "but it is not ...

42

important what happens to ... me when I no longer have Mercury to ... look after."

She drew a deep breath.

Then she said with what the Earl knew was a tremendous effort of self-control:

"I should not be bothering you, Sir, with my problems. You are a stranger and they are of no interest to anyone except myself. You cannot ... understand what I am feeling."

"As it happens, I do," the Earl contradicted. "Many years ago when I was a boy, I had a dog. It was given to me when it was a puppy and I brought it up myself. She was called Judith and I loved her more than I ever loved anyone in my whole life."

He paused and went on slowly:

"Judith went everywhere with me, she slept on my bed. If I was doing my lessons she sat at my feet, if I went riding she followed my pony."

He paused a moment.

The girl was listening to him and now she had raised her head and he could see the perfection of her small clear cut features silhouetted against the darkness of the trees.

She was looking at her horse and he could see that her eyes were very large and her dark eyelashes wet with tears stood out against the whiteness of her skin.

She was very pale and he thought that in some way there was a sort of shadowiness about her.

It was as if she was hardly human, not flesh and blood, but some spirit which had come from the woods and was a part of the trees and the soft green of the leaves.

"Quite unexpectedly," the Earl went on, "I learned one evening that I was to leave for London the following morning. There was no mention of Judith and I thought of course she would come with me. We had never left each other, I could not visualise life without her. It was only as I was taken by my attendants to the carriage waiting outside the front door that I was told that Judith was to stay behind."

"How cruel!" the girl exclaimed.

"They barely gave me time to say goodbye to her," the Earl continued. "They pulled my arms from round her neck and I was frantic with anxiety and fear as to what would become of her."

"And what did happen ... to her?" the girl asked.

"I have no idea," the Earl answered and his voice was hard.

"You mean you never saw her again?"

"I not only never saw her again, but I never heard what they did with her," the Earl replied.

"How terrible for you! How cruel! How utterly brutal!"

There was silence and then the girl added:

"So you do ... understand what I feel about ... Mercury."

"Yes, I understand," the Earl said.

Again there was silence until the girl said reflectively:

"I wonder which is worse: to imagine terrible things, to lie awake thinking of Judith's bewilderment or to know that Mercury is neglected, beaten, perhaps harnessed to a Mail Coach driven too fast with too heavy a burden."

"You are torturing yourself!" the Earl said. "There is every likelihood that a gentleman will buy him. He could be ridden by a Lady of Quality. Perhaps he will go to the stables of someone who understands horses."

"But how can I be ... sure?"

It was only a whisper.

"It will not help you – or Mercury – to anticipate the worst," the Earl said. "It is weak and perhaps a little cowardly."

There was a long pause before the girl answered.

"You are ... right. I am wrong to be so despondent and I am thinking only of ... myself. Mama would be ... ashamed of me."

"What is your name?" the Earl asked.

"Syringa," she answered almost indifferently as if she

was not attending to his question. "My father is Sir Hugh Melton and we live at the Manor House in the village."

She paused again as though she was thinking of something else, and suddenly she rose to her feet.

"I want to show you something. You have made me realise how foolishly I am behaving. I should not be crying, I should be praying for Mercury ... should I not?"

"Do you think that might help?" the Earl answered.

"I know it would," she answered.

She still kept her head turned away from him and she started to walk away from the clearing towards the trees on the left hand side.

"Stay here, Mercury!" the Earl heard her say to her horse as she passed him. Then she was moving ahead through the trees and surprised but curious the Earl followed her.

It was only a very short distance.

The trees suddenly came to an end and he saw that they stood on the edge of a sharp incline. The countryside lay below them stretching out green with woodland and uncultivated land towards the horizon.

Vaguely at the back of his mind, the Earl remembered that this was 'a look out', and that once when he had been small a groom had brought him here on one of their rides.

"From here," Syringa said softly, "all you can see is an empty world, with no houses and no roads. Actually they are there, but hidden. Mama used to say that this view is like our lives, stretching away into eternity and it is for us to make a pattern across it."

As she spoke she sat down on a flat stone on the very edge of the cliff which, bare of all vegetation, fell precipitously and dangerously away to some bushes far below.

The Earl stood beside her looking out. He understood what she meant, it was an empty world.

A world of trees just coming into bud, a world of beauty joining the horizon misty blue in the far distance.

"Mama would be ashamed of me," Syringa was saying softly. "I have been behaving like a coward. Now you have shown me how wrong I am, I will try to think of myself travelling through the empty world trying to make a straight path."

"And Mercury?" the Earl asked.

"I shall pray for him," she said, "I shall pray that he will find someone kind and understanding. Perhaps someone who loves him as much as I do. I shall pray every minute from now until Saturday."

"I am sure your prayers will be answered, Miss Melton."

"Do you really think that?"

She turned her face as she spoke and looked up at him and for the first time he saw her full face. He was not quite certain what he expected, but nothing quite so exquisite, so unusual.

She was not, in any way a conventional beauty and yet she was beautiful.

Her eyes still wet from her tears were enormous in a very small pointed face. It was a face that had a spiritual look about it, a face that no-one could describe merely as pretty.

He saw now why her hair had made him think she was a spirit of the woods because like water it seemed to reflect the light while having no definite colour of its own.

Her eyes were the same; they were grey and yet they held green and gold flecks in them, and her mouth was very sensitive.

He did not know that a woman could express so much emotion in her eyes or the movement of her lips.

She was sitting staring up at him as he towered above her. He had taken off his hat and his broad shoulders and handsome sun-tanned face with its lines of cynicism seemed to stand out like a painting on a ceiling against the blue of the sky behind him.

He realised that Syringa was looking at him in a strange manner.

Then she rose quickly to her feet before he could put out a hand to assist her.

"There is something else I want to show you," she said,

"something which I think will make you feel ... happier about Judith."

The Earl raised his eyebrows.

"It still hurts, does it not, when you think of her?" Syringa asked softly.

She did not wait for his reply but moved back along the way they had come. As she reached the clearing she called her horse.

"Mercury!"

The horse raised its head from the grass and walked towards her, and without touching him she turned into the wood. Almost immediately they came upon the Earl's stallion, Thunderer.

She saw he was tethered and waited while the Earl untied the bridle. Then she sprang into the saddle without assistance.

The Earl looked at her and thought that in her green gown mounted on the big horse she looked unreal – a fairy tale creature of dreams.

She was waiting for him, and when he was astride Thunderer she set off ahead, winding her way through the wood, going deeper and deeper towards the heart of it.

The Earl realised that the trees were getting closer together and suddenly in front of them he saw a thick thorn hedge.

It was so thick and so high he could not see how it was possible for them to penetrate it, and he expected Syringa to turn to the left or to the right.

Instead she went nearly up to the hedge and dismounted.

The Earl did the same and having again tethered Thunderer to a tree, turned expectantly towards Syringa.

"Follow me," she said in a quiet voice.

She walked towards the hedge and to the Earl's surprise found an almost impossible path which could not have been made by human feet.

Without either of them scratching themselves, twisting

47

this way and that in a curious pattern, they passed through the hedge.

It was not as thick as it looked and suddenly to the Earl's astonishment they were free of it and stepped into an open space.

There was a stretch of short green grass ahead like a lawn.

It appeared to be entirely surrounded with bushes, holly, thorns and trees.

Yet in the centre it was clear except for some fallen masonry. The Earl saw a broken pillar, then glanced towards the end of the clearing and understood.

This was the remains of one of the chapels built by the monks when there was a monastery on the site of King's Keep. The walls knocked down by the Cromwellian troops had long been over grown with ivy and honeysuckle, and giant yews growing round it had extended their branches and inter-woven them to make a thick green shield for he holy place.

But there was still the skeleton remains of what had once been a great East window and below it a huge marble slab that must have been the Altar.

The three steps leading up to the Altar were thick with mosses and lichens, the colour of coral, saffron and jade, while the forest had encroached until the Sanctuary was encircled by wild cherry and crab-apple trees rising above an undergrowth of roses, hawthorn and 'old man's beard'.

They were not yet in flower but in the clearing the Earl saw there were great clusters of primroses, their little yellow faces turned towards the light.

There were also small wild daffodils, white and purple violets and the delicate white celandine, the first flower of spring.

Syringa and the Earl stood side by side for a moment before she said very softly in a voice that was hardly above a whisper:

"There is a legend that the monks of a great Monastery

built this Chapel to the glory of St. Francis – the patron saint of the wild animals and the birds. And they say when winters are very bad the animals come here and never go away hungry."

The Earl did not speak and after a moment Syringa continued:

"I have seen birds with broken wings or dragging a leg, animals which have been mauled by a fox, and they have stayed here until they have either died in peace or have been healed. They have not been afraid of even me."

Still the Earl did not speak and she put her hand on his arm.

"I am sure," she said softly, "that if Judith could not find you, if she had been alone and fearful, she would have found her way here."

There were tears in the large grey eyes, tears of compassion, and then, as if she had no more to say, Syringa turned and wended her way back through the thorn hedge into the wood.

Mercury was waiting and the Earl untied Thunderer and led him to Syringa's side. She looked up at him and he sensed that she was worried in case he had not understood what she had shown him.

"I am honoured that you should have brought me here," he said gently.

"No-one knows about it except me," Syringa said and then with a smile, "except of course the birds and animals of Monk's Wood."

Almost with a start the Earl remembered that that was the name of the wood. It was marked on the big maps that were hung up in the Estate Office.

"I will keep your secret," he promised.

"I knew I could trust you with it."

"Why did you think that?"

"Because you ... have helped me," Syringa answered. "You have helped me more than I can ever explain, and so I must ... thank you."

"You have already thanked me," he said in his deep voice. "When I think of Judith I shall be sure that she found her way to your secret place."

"I am sure she did," Syringa agreed. "Animals are much more sensible than we are where their instincts are concerned ... especially dogs."

"And yet you trusted me."

A smile touched Syringa's lips.

"I used my instinct – something I have lamentably failed to do this past week since I learnt about the ... Sale."

Her voice trembled for a moment and then she went on :

"And now I am going to be brave about it. I shall remember the lesson you have taught me this afternoon and I will not be so frightened as I have been up till now."

"I am sure that the gods will hear your pleas," the Earl said.

He saw a startled look come into her eyes.

"Why do you look so surprised?" he asked.

A faint blush came into her cheeks.

"It is just that when I first looked at you," she answered, "you were standing above me. I saw you against the sky and it seemed to me that you were like a god. A god coming to help me."

"Which god in particular?" the Earl asked.

"Jupiter," Syringa answered instantly. "Of course you would be Jupiter, the god of the sky, the god to whom the Romans turned for protection and help in all their troubles."

"You flatter me," the Earl remarked dryly.

"I am not trying to do that," Syringa answered in all sincerity. "You have helped me, you have given me a little of your wisdom and so I shall think of you while I pray for Mercury and hope that Jupiter as well as the God of St. Francis will hear my prayer!"

"I am sure whatever prayer you make it will be heard," the Earl replied.

He had untied his horse and now he stood for a moment the reins in his hand.

"Goodbye, Syringa. If we do not meet again remember that however lonely one may feel there is always someone somewhere ready to listen."

"I will remember that," she said seriously, "and thank you, Lord Jupiter, for coming to my help when I most needed it."

She smiled up at him as she spoke.

She looked very small and fragile, little more than a child and it seemed to the Earl as if she merged into the shadows underneath the pine trees.

Almost without meaning to do so, he put his fingers under her chin, bent his head and kissed her lips.

It was the kiss of a man for a child and her lips, very soft and sweet, were as defenceless as a child's might have been. Yet just for a moment they were both very still.

Then the Earl mounted Thunderer and raising his hat, turned his horse's head in the direction of the Castle and rode away leaving Syringa staring after him.

She stood for a long time among the tree trunks until he was out of sight and she could no longer hear the sound of Thunderer's hoofs.

Then putting her arms round Mercury she hid her face against his neck.

# Chapter Three

"Now eat your breakfast, Miss Syringa, and no nonsense!" Nurse said in the severe tones of one who is used to recreant nursery charges.

"I am trying," Syringa answered.

But as she spoke she knew she could not force anything down her throat which seemed to have swollen twice its normal size.

She rose from the table and walked to the window to look out onto the small untended garden with its chestnut trees and its huge bushes of syringa.

They were just coming into bud and she thought miserably that by the time they were in flower she would have left the house and would never see them again.

She turned her head to see her nurse had laid the breakfast tray for her father.

"I will take it up to him, Nana," she said quietly.

"I don't suppose Sir Hugh will eat anything," Nurse replied slipping some pieces of toast onto a silver rack. "And if he doesn't want to, bring the tray down again. The coffee set and all the rest of the silver is in the Sale."

Syringa did not answer but merely carried the neatly arranged tray, with its lace-edged cloth and pretty flower-decorated china, up the stairs to set it down on the table outside the door of the main bed-room.

She knocked on the door but there was no answer, and after knocking again she picked up the tray and went in.

She could see in the dim light her father was not asleep

but lying back against the pillows, his arms behind his head.

"Good morning, Papa," Syringa said, "I have brought you some breakfast."

"I do not want any."

Sir Hugh's voice was thick, the words slightly blurred.

And Syringa, even before she noticed the half-empty decanter of brandy on the table beside the bed, knew he had already been drinking.

She set down the tray and walked to the window to pull back the curtains and let in the pale sunshine.

"A cup of coffee will do you good, Papa," she said tentatively, knowing that sometimes any suggestion as to what he should eat or drink would make Sir Hugh turn on her in a rage.

This morning he merely reached out his hand towards the decanter.

"I am sure it would," he said, "but I am not concerned this morning with what is good or bad for me."

Syringa, feeling that he was in a more mellow mood than she had expected, decided to ask the question which had been hovering in her mind ever since she had learnt about the Sale.

"If you do not think it impertinent of me, Papa," she said, "will you tell me exactly how much you owe?"

It seemed to Syringa that her inquisitiveness evoked a pregnant silence.

Then as Sir Hugh poured out half a glass of brandy with a shaky hand he said:

"So you are curious, are you? Well I do not blame you! You may as well know the worst and have done with it. I owe twenty thousand pounds!"

As he finished speaking he tipped the glass of brandy down his throat and threw himself back against the pillows and closed his eyes.

For a moment Syringa was too horrified to speak, then at last in a voice which seemed to her curiously unlike her own, she ejaculated:

"Twenty thousand pounds! But, Papa, how could we ... ever find so ... such a sum?"

Sir Hugh opened his eyes.

"We have to! Do you hear me? And ten thousand is a debt of honour that must be paid first."

"But, Papa," Syringa expostulated, "the gentleman to whom you owe so much would not put you in prison. While the others ..."

"Be quiet!" Sir Hugh said sharply. "I may be a fool, Syringa, I may be a damned bad gamester, but I am still a gentleman. I still honour my word."

He paused and then staring at her angrily he added:

"Stop thinking like some parsimonious cheese-paring tradesman. Why should not shop-keepers wait for their money? Curse it, that is all they are good for!"

"They have waited a long time, Papa," Syringa said softly.

"And they will wait a damn sight longer," Sir Hugh snarled.

He suddenly put up his hands to his eyes.

"Draw the curtains, blast you!" he exclaimed. "What do you want to let in all this light for? My head aches and if I have to face those ravening wolves downstairs, I need another bottle of brandy."

"That was the last bottle, Papa," Syringa answered.

"The last bottle!" Sir Hugh ejaculated the words as though he felt he could not have heard her aright. "Are you sure?"

"Quite sure, Papa. It was the only bottle left in the cellar. I looked yesterday."

Sir Hugh turned to look at the now almost empty decanter.

"God! How do you expect me to get through today without something to drink?" he demanded.

"I have brought you some coffee, Papa."

"Coffee!" Sir Hugh roared, "I want brandy and I am curst well going to have it! Get my shaving-water and bring me my boots. I suppose that lazy old nurse of yours has cleaned them."

"Yes, Papa, Nana has cleaned them. And she has washed one of your best shirts and I have ironed it for you," Syringa said. "Your coat has been sponged and pressed."

She drew a deep breath.

"Please, Papa, do not drink any more," she pleaded. "If you have to face the people coming to the Sale, I want them to see how smart and handsome you are when you are not..."

She paused.

"Drunk as a lord!" her father finished bitterly, "jug-bitten, bosky, foxed, any word you like to call it. It just means degraded, debauched, a man you have no reason to be proud of as your father."

His voice was so sharp with pain that instinctively Syringa went towards him. She put her hand and laid it on his which lay against the sheet.

"I am sorry, Papa," she said. "You know I would help you if I could."

"I know that," her father said in a very different tone of voice. "You are a good girl, Syringa, your mother would have been proud of you."

As he spoke of his wife Sir Hugh's voice softened and suddenly there were weak tears in his bloodshot eyes.

"It is all because I miss Elizabeth," he whimpered. "I cannot live without her, I never could live without her. How could she have died and left me alone, how could she, Syringa?"

This was a familiar cry and Syringa knew when her father's drinking had passed the aggressive stage and he became maudlin and sentimental.

"This would never have happened if your mother had still been here," he went on almost as if he was speaking to himself. "She kept me from making a fool of myself and made me behave decently. Oh, Syringa, how could I have failed her?"

The tears were running now down Sir Hugh's cheeks and there was compassion in Syringa's eyes as she looked at him, but she knew it was only a passing mood.

A few more drinks and he would be aggressive again, cursing the tradesmen, ready to post back to London if he had any money to throw it away in drink and gaming.

"I will fetch your shaving-water, Papa," she said and was moving from the bedside when she remembered his breakfast.

She poured the black coffee into a thin porcelain cup.

"Please drink this, Papa," she urged. "It will steady you and make you feel stronger."

"Stronger for what?" her father asked. "I am hopeless and there is no point in my going on living."

"Please, Papa, drink the coffee," Syringa coaxed.

Still muttering to himself, Sir Hugh lifted the cup to his lips, drank a little, then said in disgust:

"Tastes like bilge water! What I want is brandy!"

"Then you must get up," Syringa replied.

She picked up the tray as she spoke and went from the room. Her father was in a bad state this morning she thought dispassionately, as she went downstairs.

At first, after her mother's death three years ago, she had been desperately disturbed and distressed by his drunkenness, his violent moods of aggression when at times he even knocked her about.

It was almost worse when he repented, when he wept and begged her forgiveness, when he re-iterated over and over again how much he missed his wife.

But she had learnt through bitter experience that it was all an act.

However repentant her father might be one moment, if he had a few guineas in his hand he would throw them away.

Without a thought of the consequences, without remembering that she and her old Nurse, who had been in his service ever since he married, were often on the point of

56

starvation, he would go back to the gaming tables.

It had been horrible too to realise that his craving for drink was more insistent and more important to him than even his memories of her mother.

He had sold the small pieces of jewellery that Lady Melton had treasured and which she had always told Syringa were to be hers.

The money he had obtained for them had gone in one evening of debauchery, and sometimes Syringa felt she could never forgive her father for treating her mother's possessions so indifferently.

There was very little of any value in the house, because ever since her father and mother had run away together, they had lived on the very small fortune her mother had inherited when she was twenty-one.

It amounted to only a few hundred pounds a year and yet it enabled them to be comparatively comfortable so long as they were not extravagant.

As Syringa grew up, she had learnt that her father must have everything of the best.

It was her father who must have a decent horse to ride and to go hunting, even if her mother's shoes had holes in them and her gowns were threadbare.

Her father had the whole attention of the three women in the house.

Syringa soon learnt to play her part in seeing that he was dressed like a dandy, even though her own dress was so outgrown as to be almost indecent.

Yet she could understand why her mother never regretted leaving her family in the North who had planned for her to marry a wealthy Scottish nobleman.

She had chosen instead to live in what they considered penury with a man who had nothing to recommend him save his good looks and his devotion which had kept his wife blissfully happy for all the years of their married life.

Syringa had realised, when she was old enough to think of grown-ups as human beings, that it was her mother who kept the house together and made her father so content that he did not mind their comparative poverty.

It was her mother who made every hour that Sir Hugh spent at home as amusing and as entertaining as if he was with the rowdy friends who had been his companions when he was a bachelor.

It was only as she grew older that Syringa realised that her father missed the amusements he had known in London.

He longed sometimes for his clubs which he could no longer afford and the comradeship of men like himself who had few interests beyond sport and gambling.

As she looked back on the days before her mother died, Syringa felt that it was by using her brain and her intelligence that her mother had kept her husband at her side.

He had been content – there was no doubt about it.

Content with the life they lived at Whitley, content with the confinement of the small Manor House, content with the wife who loved him to the exclusion of everything else in the world.

But on her death, sudden and unexpected, her father had behaved like a madman.

It seemed as if the repressions of the years in which he had behaved normally, in which he had been a good husband and a good father, had built up inside him.

When disaster came it broke the banks of his self-control and he no longer had any restraint over his emotions or his desires.

He had rushed away to London the moment his wife had been lowered into the grave and had not returned for three months.

When he came back Syringa hardly recognised him.

It had taken him less than a year to become so debauched and so depraved, and sometimes she prayed that he would not return to the house and terrify her.

Then she learnt to handle him.

Not as skilfully as her mother had done, that would have

been impossible, because although he was fond of her she could not control him, she could not prevent him from drinking himself into unconsciousness whenever he had the chance.

It was soon obvious that Sir Hugh only returned home when his money had run out, or when he had become so incoherent with drink that even his cronies were bored with him.

Syringa would nurse him back to health.

It was not an easy thing to do but somehow she achieved it, mostly because Sir Hugh could not afford the brandy for which his body now craved incessantly.

Sometimes they were without any money until her father found that he could raise a loan from a friend.

Then he would post to London and Syringa would realise despondently that all her efforts had been in vain.

When he returned she would have to start again.

Entering the kitchen, Syringa set her father's uneaten breakfast down on the table.

Nana glanced at it and said:

"I knew it would be a waste of time. Is he getting up?"

"I said I would take Papa his shaving-water," Syringa answered.

Without comment the old Nurse poured some boiling water into a silver jug.

Syringa put it on a silver salver and picking up a white shirt with lace-edged cuffs that was airing in front of the fire, she walked up-stairs again.

Her father was lying in the same position as she had left him, his hands over his eyes, but she noted that the decanter was now completely empty.

She put his shaving-water on the washhand-stand, laid his shirt over a chair and fetched from the wardrobe his white breeches and well-cut coat with its long tails.

Nana had left Sir Hugh's highly polished Hessian boots outside the door the night before.

They had taken her over an hour to clean, but now they

shone brightly as any Dandy's might have done, and Syringa set them down near the chair.

"What is the time?" her father asked when she was preparing to leave the room.

"It is about half past eight, Papa. The Sale starts at ten, but I expect people will be arriving soon after nine to inspect the house. So you had best be clear of this room so that Nana and I can make the bed."

"What is the point of making it? I am not going to sleep in it again," Sir Hugh growled.

"It will look tidier," Syringa answered. "I would not wish strangers to think we were slovenly or careless in our ways."

"What the hell does it matter what strangers think?" Sir Hugh asked. "They will be walking about my house, fingering my possessions, taking them away in their carts and carriages."

"And when they have gone where do we go, Papa?" Syringa asked quietly. "Have you made any plans?"

There was silence before her father replied surlily:

"You will learn in good time what I have planned."

Syringa knew as he spoke that really he had no idea what they would do or what would become of them.

She had the sudden uneasy feeling that when the moment came they would be turned out of the Manor just to walk the roads, to sleep in a ditch.

Then mentally she shook herself. It could not be as bad as that – it could not be – or could it?

She ran down the stairs as if to escape from her own thoughts and out to the stable.

Mercury heard her coming and he was whinnying before she could open the stable-door. She went inside and he nuzzled his nose against her.

"Oh, Mercury! Mercury!" Syringa cried, "I have been praying for you all night. Praying that you will find a happy home with people who will be kind to you and love you as I do."

The great horse pushed his nose against her cheek. She kissed him, her arms going round his neck.

But her eyes were dry, she was past tears – past everything, she thought, but the urge to pray as she had been praying during the last few days that, whatever happened to her, Mercury would not suffer.

She wondered if there was time to ride her horse once again and knew there was not.

There were still a dozen things to be arranged in the house. She and Nana had set the chairs in the dining-room and the Auctioneer had brought a stand for himself and a desk from which he could take the bids.

He had made a catalogue of the contents of the house and Syringa, going round with him, had felt ashamed that so many of the things were broken or damaged.

It had been impossible to explain to the dry uninterested man that they had not been able to afford to have things repaired.

She and her mother had done their best to hold together the antique furniture, to patch the curtains and replace the webbing when it sagged under the chairs.

She knew that the Auctioneer disparaged not only the furniture but the pictures that were badly in need of revarnishing or reframing, and the silver, which, while it looked bright from Nana's frequent polishings, was not old enough to be of any great value.

Nevertheless it seemed to Syringa that by the time he had finished he had quite an impressive list of items to be sold.

At the top there was the house itself, at the bottom the last item of the sale – was Mercury.

"That horse is the best of the lot," the Auctioneer said, "and if we put him last, it will encourage those who are interested in him to stay until the end. That is important. We do not want them driving away too soon, that lowers the price quicker than anything."

"The best of the lot," Syringa whispered now to herself, and opened the stable-door.

"Come, Mercury, let us go for a walk."

She led the horse away from the house into the paddock.

The grass was damp from dew, and lifting up her skirts a little Syringa walked across the field to where there was a tiny copse in which she had often hidden as a child.

She had a wild impulse to hide there with Mercury and not to go back.

The Sale would start without them. At first no-one would realise that she was not there or that the horse was missing, and when they came to the last item . . .

Syringa shook her head. No, she could not do it! It would be too despicable and would be a betrayal not only of her father but of her mother's trust in her.

She knew that her mother would want her above all things to look after the man she had loved so deeply and who had meant everything in the world to her.

"I have tried . . . Mama . . . I have tried!" Syringa whispered and held her breath as if expecting her mother to answer her.

She must somehow feel that her mother was near, understanding, helping, guiding her to do the right thing.

Then despondently she thought she could feel nothing except the soft breeze on her cheeks and the sound of Mercury following behind her.

She had often called aloud to her mother since her death, even as her father called out in his drunkenness, believing she must be hiding somewhere in the house.

But there had only been silence for both of them.

Syringa reached the copse and stood for a moment with her back against one of the trees staring at the Manor.

It looked small, grey and rather insignificant, and yet it was the only home she had ever known, the only place to which she belonged. In an hour's time that too would be gone!

Mercury was waiting, surprised that his mistress was walking when she might be riding and perhaps even instinctively knowing something was wrong.

Syringa bent and kissed his nose.

"I love you," she said, "I love you and there is nothing more I can do except to go on praying for you for the rest of your life."

When they returned to the stable Syringa rubbed Mercury down.

She had brushed him the night before and combed his mane and she knew that he had never looked more handsome.

She had just finished bringing him hay and water when she heard voices outside and saw some strange men coming into the stable-yard.

She knew then, with a sudden pain in her heart that was almost like the turn of a dagger, that these were people who were attending the sale and who perhaps intended to bid for Mercury.

In a sudden panic, knowing she could not speak to them, could not enumerate the good points of her horse, Syringa ran from the stall and crossing the yard entered the house by a side door. She ran upstairs to change her dress realising that the one she wore was damp round the hem and that her feet were also wet.

She had just finished arranging a clean white muslin fichu round her shoulders when Nana came into her bed-room.

"Your father is asking for you, Miss Syringa."

"Is he all right?"

There was no need for Nana to ask what Syringa meant.

"He tried to borrow some money from me but I could tell him truthfully that I had none," Nana replied. "So he takes it from the first person who arrives at the Sale. It happened to be old Farmer Proger."

"So he has ... some more ... brandy," Syringa said almost beneath her breath.

"He is in his Study," Nana said abruptly and went from the room.

Syringa did not bother to glance at herself in the mirror. She hurried downstairs and as she reached the hall saw that the Dining-room was already packed with people.

They were sitting in rows looking, she thought, like vultures waiting for the pickings.

She recognised several familiar faces and yet there were an enormous number of strangers, middle-aged men neatly and unobtrusively dressed.

For a moment she could not place them, and then she recognised one man whom she had seen before.

He had come to the Manor from London demanding that her father pay his wine bill. It was for a very large sum, but her father was not at home and Syringa could do nothing but send the man away.

She saw him now sitting in the third row.

She knew then that all the other strangers, the men who seemed somehow out of place amongst the farmers and the villagers, were all tradesmen – men to whom her father was in debt, men who, if their bills were not met, could send him to prison.

She ran as if pursued by a sudden terror into the study.

Her father was sitting in a wing-backed armchair, a glass of brandy in his hand.

"Papa, there are a lot of your creditors here," Syringa said in a frightened voice.

"Of course there are!" Sir Hugh said, "and I say to them, come! Let them all come! Let them bid, let them buy, let them give me their money!"

"You do not understand, Papa. They will not buy anything. They have only come to collect the money as soon as the Sale is over."

"God damn it!" Sir Hugh ejaculated. "I might be a fox with the hounds after me! Well I hope I give them a good run for their money. They have chased me long enough, but they have not got me yet!"

Syringa sighed. She realised that her father was too drunk to understand, too drunk to realise the seriousness of what was happening.

She had left the door slightly ajar when she entered the

64

room, and now she heard the dull rap of a hammer and the general chatter suddenly ceased.

Then the Auctioneer's rather precise voice began:

"Good morning, Gentlemen. The first item on our catalogue is ..."

With a swift movement Syringa shut the door.

She could not bear it, could not bear to hear the man mouthing over her home, her possessions, everything that she had known and loved since she was a child.

She tried to pretend it was all a dream and it was not really happening.

But always at the back of her mind she had known the day must come when her father would not be able to continue living on credit, piling up debts, borrowing from his friends.

Yet she had hoped against hope that he would have a lucky winning streak, or would reform and change back into the decent, affectionate man he had been when her mother was alive.

It was a child's dream, she thought now, something which bore no resemblance to reality.

She stood for a long time, not looking at her father, but hearing the clink of the bottle against the glass as he poured himself drink after drink.

Then the door was opened and two men in white aprons came in to take three chairs into the auction room. They returned to remove a table and two pictures from the walls.

Syringa moved to sit in the window-seat. She must have been there for over an hour before the two men came back into the room and looked uncertainly at Sir Hugh.

"Could we 'ave the chair you're a sitting on, Gov'nor?" they asked. "'Tis wanted."

"What is wanted?" Sir Hugh asked in a thick voice.

"The chair, Gov'nor. 'Tis to be sold."

Sir Hugh opened his mouth to curse them, but Syringa moved swiftly to his side.

"There is no point, Papa," she said quietly, "they are only

65

doing their duty. Come and sit in the window."

She picked up the decanter as she spoke and took the glass from his hand. One of the men put out a hand and helped her father to his feet.

As they went from the room carrying the wing-backed chair, Sir Hugh stood looking after them.

"I have sat in that chair ever since I lived here."

"I know, Papa," Syringa answered, "and now it is to be sold."

"Your mother was very fond of that chair."

"Do not think about it," Syringa began.

She thought with a feeling of despair that at any moment he would become maudlin.

She thought she could not bear the people they knew, let alone a collection of strangers, to see him cry or hear him humiliate himself as he did so often to her.

Hastily in her anxiety, Syringa poured a little more brandy into a glass.

"Come, Papa," she said, "as you have bought this, you might as well drink it."

Her father raised the glass to his lips. Then he said in a low voice as if he spoke to himself.

"I have seen the debtor's cells in Newgate – they are dark, and evil. The stench remained in my nostrils for days."

He drank again and went on :

"The prisoners are like wild animals – their shrieks echo round the walls – they fight for food as if they were starving. How can I face such conditions, such ghastly degradation?"

There was sheer horror in his tone.

"Perhaps it will be all right, Papa," Syringa suggested soothingly. "The sale may make enough money to pay off all your debts."

She knew as she spoke it was a forlorn hope. How could the house and furniture fetch so vast a sum?

"How can I endure Newgate?" Sir Hugh asked, his voice

thick with emotion and drink. "Gaol Fever kills hundreds of prisoners a year. I shall have no money with which to buy comforts and must herd with those who live like animals!"

"Do not torture yourself, Papa," Syringa pleaded, "perhaps your creditors will give you more time."

"And what is to become of you?" Sir Hugh asked, as if she had not spoken. "What have I done, Syringa?"

"It is too late to worry about it now, Papa."

"What would your mother have thought, if she had seen our possessions going under the hammer, our home sold over our heads?"

There was a note of panic in her father's voice and Syringa rose to her feet.

"Come and sit down, Papa," she said, "nothing can be changed at this late hour."

"What is happening?" Sir Hugh asked. "I have to know what is happening! Come, Syringa, we will listen to the bids."

"No, Papa, no," Syringa begged.

Ignoring her, he reached out his hand and took her by the arm propelling her along beside him.

He pulled her across the hall and they entered the Auction room.

The chair Sir Hugh recently vacated was standing just inside the door. Another chair that had been sold earlier was beside it, and still holding Syringa by the arm her father sat down and pulled her down beside him.

One of the men in a white apron was holding up a picture off the stairs.

It was of a man on a white horse, and Syringa had loved it when she was a small child.

"Five guineas I am bid?" the Auctioneer said. "Five – six – seven – eight ... Any advance on eight? What about you, Sir? The bidding is against you."

The man he looked at shook his head.

"Then at eight guineas. It is going cheap, Gentlemen. Going ..."

"Nine guineas," someone said at the back.

Syringa could not see who spoke because there were a number of people standing who could not get a seat.

"Nine guineas," the Auctioneer said. "Any advance on nine guineas? Going – going – gone! Sold to the same gentleman," he said in a quiet voice to his clerk who was sitting beside him.

They were now almost at the end of the Sale, Syringa thought.

The carpets had been sold, the furniture, and now there were only a few things left from the garden. A wooden seat on which she had often sat with her mother, a roller and a wheelbarrow.

These were all disposed of for quite small sums, except, Syringa noticed, that when the bidding came to a stop it was always the same voice at the end of the room who put the price up higher still.

"And now we come to perhaps the most important item in the catalogue," the Auctioneer said, "and one for which I know a number of you Gentlemen have been waiting."

He smiled as he spoke showing his false teeth, and Syringa clasping her hands together felt as if it was hard to breathe.

"It is something we cannot bring into the Sale room," the Auctioneer continued jovially, "but I know that most of you will have seen it outside. A fine piece of horseflesh. A five year old stallion broken to the saddle and used to carrying a lady on his back, and a pretty lady too."

He smiled and went on.

"Sixteen hands in height, sound in wind and limb and altogether an animal that would fetch a competitive price in any Sale. Who will start me off at sixty guineas?"

There was silence.

"Well, make a suggestion, gentlemen."

"Thirty," someone said almost grudgingly.

"Ridiculous!" the Auctioneer exclaimed. "Very well then, thirty guineas – forty – fifty – sixty. Against you, Sir.

Seventy – seventy guineas I am bid. What advance on seventy? It is cheap at the price, Gentlemen, you would pay far more at the local horse fair. That I can assure you."

He paused and looked round.

"Seventy guineas, a magnificent animal, in the prime of life, quiet, easy to handle, a lady's mount and yet well capable of carrying a gentleman all day in the hunting field without showing exhaustion. Seventy guineas – any advance on seventy?"

"Seventy-five," a voice said.

Syringa looked quickly to see a farmer she most disliked, a man she always suspected of being as hard on his horse as he was on his employees.

"Oh no! Please God, not him," she prayed. "Please God!"

"Seventy-five guineas," the Auctioneer said. "Any other bid? No advance on seventy-five? Very well – going . . ."

"I cannot bear it," Syringa thought, "I cannot bear Mercury to go to that man."

"A hundred guineas," a voice said from the back.

With a sudden gasp every head in the room turned to look at the last speaker.

"Thank you, Sir," the Auctioneer said, "thank you very much. A hundred guineas! Any other bids? Very well then, going – going – gone!"

Syringa craned her neck.

It was the same quiet voice that had spoken before. She could not see the man. He was lost in the crowd and she felt too embarrassed to stand up.

"I must talk to him," she thought, "I must tell him about Mercury . . . I must ask him to be kind to him."

And then her attention was recalled to what was happening.

"That concludes the Sale, gentlemen," the Auctioneer said.

"How much? How much has it made?"

A voice came from the hall and then was taken up by several others.

"Yes, tell us!"

"Let's know the full amount!"

"What's the tally?"

There was something hostile in the questions and the Auctioneer bent his head to consult with his clerk.

"This is rather irregular, Gentlemen," he said. "I have not yet disclosed the proceeds of the Sale to the previous owner."

He looked towards Sir Hugh as he spoke.

"Then tell him," someone suggested. "He can't be too drunk or too deaf to hear that!"

Syringa looked apprehensively at her father. As if he realised what was taking place, Sir Hugh rose unsteadily to his feet.

"Very well," he said in an aggressive tone. "Let us have the accounting here and now, if that is what pleases you."

He turned to the Auctioneer.

"How much has this rabble paid for my prize possessions?"

They jeered and laughed at this, and the Auctioneer again consulting with his clerk said:

"I make it a little under ten thousand pounds, Sir Hugh."

"Ten thousand," Sir Hugh repeated reflectively.

There was silence and then the Auctioneer, in a voice which he meant to be low, but which somehow was perfectly audible in the hall, said:

"You will remember, Sir Hugh, that amount is owed to Sir Percy Grayson and Lord Cloverdale."

"I am well aware of that, my man," Sir Hugh said. "See that they receive the money due to them."

As he finished speaking there was a sudden yell of fury.

It was almost like the sound of wild animals baying, and the men who had sat quietly through the auction came surging up to the stand like a great wave of the sea, knocking over the chairs as they did so.

"'Tis our money," one man shouted, "we're entitled to it,

it's ours. You pay up and pay us first. That's what we've come for."

There were shouts from the others and Syringa saw that they were all pulling bills from their pockets, long curling pieces of parchment with Sir Hugh's debts to them written in neat script.

"Pay! Pay! Pay!"

One of the men started to chant the words and now they all took it up.

"Pay! Pay! Pay us, pay us!"

For a moment Sir Hugh stood bewildered and then with an effort he straightened his shoulders and put up his chin.

"I regret, Gentlemen," he said, "that my pockets are to let. You cannot have what I do not possess."

"Then 'tis prison for you, me fine Gentleman!" one man screamed.

"That's right, put him in the debtor's prison, that is where he belongs," another cried.

It seemed to Syringa they were like dogs snapping and snarling at her father. Because she was afraid for him she went to his side and put her hands on his arm.

"Come away, Papa, there is nothing you can do."

"Pay! Pay!" the men were chanting. "Prison! Take him to prison! Get the bailiffs!"

Syringa's hand tightened on her father's arm.

There was something bestial and unrestrained in the cries and yells from the men she was facing.

Then suddenly Sir Hugh put his arm round her shoulder.

"Here is my last possession, Gentlemen," he said. "You have had everything else from me, what do you bid for my daughter?"

Syringa glanced up at her father in consternation.

He was very drunk she realised, drunker than she had thought when he had risen from the chair. She knew him so well that she realised he had reached a wild state when he would say or do anything.

A state when he would defy the fates, when he felt himself immune from the consequences of his own action.

"Papa! Please Papa!" she begged.

Sir Hugh did not hear her. He was facing his accusers with a smile on his lips and defiance in his eyes.

"Shy?" he sneered, "come on, speak up!"

The men were hushed into silence.

"Are you too chicken-hearted to take my last possession from me? You have taken everything else. Go on, have the lot! She must be worth something on the open market. Young, untouched, a good wife for an honest man. Bid for her, you swine!"

There was silence.

Then from the back of the hall where a crowd of the villagers and farmers still stood staring in bewilderment at the noise and turmoil around the hall, a quiet voice said:

"Ten thousand pounds."

There was a gasp, an audible sound which seemed to echo and repeat itself.

Almost automatically the Auctioneer resumed his rightful place.

"Did you say ten thousand pounds, Sir?" he asked. "Ten thousand pounds, I am bid. Any advance on ten thousand?"

There was only silence and then the hammer came down.

"Going – going – gone!"

Syringa gave a little cry.

"Papa, you cannot mean it!"

Her father took his arm from her and pushed her to one side, forcing his way through the crowd of creditors staring at him open-mouthed. Then walking unsteadily across the hall, he went into the study and slammed the door behind him.

Syringa made as if to follow him, but she could not do so because the crowd of men besieging the Auctioneer almost swept her off her feet.

"Pay us! Pay us!" they were crying.

The Auctioneer's voice was shrill but still authoritative above the uproar.

"You will all be paid, Gentlemen – all of you – if you will wait your turn."

His words calmed the mob and at last Syringa could move.

Then even as she pushed her way towards the hall, there was an explosion, the loud echoing report of a pistol shot, and she knew what had happened!

# Chapter Four

Nurse put an egg down on the table in front of Syringa who looked up with a question in her eyes.

"Where did this come from?"

"Mrs. Geary let me have half a dozen," Nurse answered.

"You mean she gave you credit!" Syringa cried. "Oh, Nana, you know we cannot do that."

Her old Nurse put her hands on her hips.

"Now listen to me, Miss Syringa. If you think I'm going to stand here and watch you starve yourself to death, you're mistaken! We have lived on potatoes and bits of vegetables for the last two weeks and I for one'll put up with no more of it."

She paused, and as Syringa did not answer she went on :

"Not even a leaf of tea. I never thought the time would come when I couldn't have a cup of tea, and that's a fact!"

"Oh, I know, Nana," Syringa said miserably, "it is worse for you than it is for me. But we cannot run up debts, you must see that."

"And who is going to notice a few shillings?" Nurse asked fiercely. "Not His Lordship, who is too high and mighty to call on us or to leave the gay lights in London for the boredom of the countryside."

"Why should he bother about us?" Syringa asked. "It must have been a mistake his agent bidding for me like that."

Her voice was low almost as if she spoke to herself, and then looking at the brown egg in front of her she automatically picked up her apron.

"That's right, eat it while it's hot," her Nurse said. "You know as well as I do that you're hungry even if your pride'll not let you admit it."

"Of course I am hungry," Syringa answered, as she broke off the top of the egg and took a spoonful. "But we have no right to pledge his Lordship's credit."

She took another spoonful and then asked quickly:

"You have had an egg yourself, Nana?"

"I have, and I'm not ashamed of it!" Nurse answered. "I am getting on for sixty and I've never had to work without food in my life, and I'm not going to start now."

She watched Syringa eating the egg with satisfaction then said:

"Mrs. Geary is still willing to buy the mirror. She'll pay up to three pounds for it, and three pounds would buy us a lot of food."

"It is not ours to sell," Syringa answered. "You know that."

"Do you imagine His Lordship would miss one carved mirror when he owns King's Keep?"

"He paid for it and it is his," Syringa answered. "Whether he knows about it or not, I cannot be dishonest."

The Nurse snorted and Syringa went on:

"We are of no consequence to someone of such importance, but at the same time I wish to keep my self-respect. And I will not, Nana, I will not run into debt."

Nurse knew she was thinking of her father and her face softened.

"I don't want to do anything to upset you, dearie," she said, "but you knows we can't go on as we are. Let me send a message to King's Keep to find out when the Earl is returning."

Her eyes were worried.

"I can't watch you awasting away in front of my very eyes."

Syringa did not answer and after a moment Nurse continued:

75

"Supposing he never comes to see us? I've been finding out about the Earl of Rothingham this last week or so. There are many tales about him and none to his advantage."

"What sort of tales?" Syringa asked slowly.

She spoke almost reluctantly as if the words were forced between her lips.

She had finished the egg and she rose from the table as she spoke.

There was nothing else to eat, no bread, no butter, and her only drink for the last few days had been a little honey and warm water. Now the honey had come to an end.

"Of course," Nana began, "few have seen His Lordship because he didn't come into the house until the Colonel died. They say he's not like his father – that's a blessing at any rate!"

"Was the last Earl very bad?" Syringa enquired.

"You've heard your father speak of him," Nana replied, "he couldn't come home after the Colonel took over. A gamester, that's what he was. He gambled away everything! Everything he could lay his hands on!"

"How terrible for his family," Syringa murmured.

"He only had one child, the present Earl," Nurse answered, "and he's been abroad for years. Though I should be surprised if he's not a chip off the old block, they all say he doesn't gamble."

"That at least must be a point in his favour," Syringa answered and shivered as she thought of her father.

"'Tis not only gaming that brings about a man's downfall," Nana snapped.

"What do you mean by that?" Syringa asked.

"There be other – things," Nana said evasively.

"What sort of things?" Syringa insisted. "What have you heard about the Earl of Rothingham that you have not heard before?"

"Well, Mrs. Geary was speaking about His Lordship this very morning," Nana replied. "It appears that Joe had taken some groceries up to the house. Very honoured she was at being invited to supply King's Keep. The Colonel never patronised shops in Whitley."

"What did she tell you?" Syringa asked.

"Joe was hearing up at the house that the Earl was a hard man. It seems that when he paid them a visit some weeks ago, His Lordship demanded a great many improvements to be made on the Estate. From what I hear, he had Mr. Archer shaking in his shoes."

"I expect things had got a little slack," Syringa said. "After all the Colonel was eighty. And he was too ill to be troubled these past five years."

She gave a little sigh.

"I miss him! He was always very kind to me and I do hope the new Earl will not alter King's Keep. It is so lovely as it is."

Her Nurse did not answer her and after a moment Syringa went on:

"They said His Lordship is a hard man and you heard other tales about him?"

"I shouldn't be gossiping," Nana said almost crossly, "but they do talk of him as being a Rake, and oh, my dear, it's worried about you I am! What'll become of you in the clutches of a man like that?"

Syringa gave a little laugh.

"You are making His Lordship into a bogey man. What can he do to me?"

She did not see the expression on her Nurse's face and continued lightly:

"The worst he can do is ask for his money back and I cannot see how even if I work for the rest of my life, I can ever make ten thousand pounds! It must have been a mistake, Nana, the Agent bidding for me like that."

"Well, if it was, it's an expensive one!" Nurse said tartly and picking up Syringa's plate she went from the room.

Syringa went from the house to the stables.

"I am not worried about myself," she thought, "so much as Nana and Mercury."

That was the real worry, Mercury! It was not good for him to eat only the new grass, he needed the oats and hay he had always had, but they had been finished for over a week.

Syringa had brushed out the granary, getting down on her hands and knees to find every tiny grain and now there was nothing left.

Mercury heard her coming and whinnied. She opened his stall and let him out. He nuzzled his nose against her and she patted his neck.

"You had better go for a run in the field," she said, "and I will groom you."

She knew really she ought to exercise him, but she had felt so tired and weak these last days, and although more than anything else she loved riding Mercury, it had been too much of an effort.

It seemed incredible that anyone living in what, compared with the villagers, was a large house with her family possessions around her, could be completely without money.

Syringa had thought that after the Sale there would be a message of some sort from the new owner, but apart from the fact that she had learnt that the purchaser was the Earl of Rothingham, she had heard nothing.

She thought at first that the absence of any communication was in consideration of her father's death.

But when the funeral was over, attended by none save a few villagers, she and Nana had gone back to the house and waited and waited without hearing anything.

At first Syringa had been almost afraid to go out riding or to leave the house in case the Earl or his representative arrived.

Then as the days went past, she began to think they must be forgotten.

It would not have mattered, she thought, except that

they had literally no money with which to buy food. The last of the chickens, which they kept to supply the house with eggs, had been killed before the Sale to make a meal for her father.

Nana had begged, borrowed and finally bought food and despite everything Syringa said she continued to do so.

There were a few vegetables in the garden: spring cabbages, some small marrows and a few very tiny new potatoes.

These fortunately had been planted earlier in the year when Sir Hugh had returned home for a short time with a little money, Syringa had persuaded him to expend a few shillings on planting vegetables in the garden and purchasing a few hens.

But now even the vegetables were finished, and Syringa realised that for Nana's sake and for Mercury's something had to be done.

She led Mercury into the paddock and leaned on the gate to watch him trotting around for a moment as if to exercise his legs and then stopping to crop the grass.

"I must do something!"

She found herself repeating the words as she walked back to the house. Even if she was prepared to hold tightly on to the only thing she had left – her pride, she could not let Nana suffer. She was too old and it might even kill her!

As she entered the hall Syringa came to a sudden decision.

"I will change my clothes," she told herself, "I will put on my riding-habit, ride to King's Keep, and ask them for news of the Earl. They must have some idea when he is visiting them again. Or perhaps I should see the agent. I think it must have been Mr. Archer who was doing the bidding."

Even as she made the decision she felt a feeling of humiliation.

It would be humiliating to tell the Earl or his employees that they could not go on as they were without food.

Would it be better, she wondered, to sell the mirror or anything else in the house?

As she thought of it, she realised how, compared with all the magnificent treasures in King's Keep, anything her father had possessed could only be classified as junk. Nevertheless they were not now hers to sell.

She had seen, after her father had shot himself, the shopkeepers who had hounded him slipping out of the house quite unconcerned because they now had their money.

She loathed the dishonesty of debt more than anything else in the world. It was dishonest to buy what you could not pay for, to obtain under false pretences what you had no chance of ever owning legally.

"It was dishonesty that killed my father," she had said to Nana.

She had said it angrily during one of their long arguments that had gone on day after day as to whether they should sell something from the house or obtain food on credit.

It had been the truth and Nana had had no answer.

But Syringa was determined that never again in the whole of her life would she buy anything unless she had the money to pay for it.

"Very high-souled sentiments!" her brain jeered at her, "which will not prevent you from feeling hungry!"

But she found it impossible to laugh at herself.

"I will go to King's Keep," Syringa said aloud, and even as she spoke she looked back through the open front door and saw a Phaeton coming up the short drive.

For a moment she stared at it wide-eyed, then she realised that the sunshine was flashing on silver harness and that the fine horseflesh were being tooled by a Gentleman in a top-hat.

She gave a little cry and ran to the kitchen.

"There is a Phaeton coming up the drive, Nana," she exclaimed. "It must be the Earl! Quick, go to the door! I will receive him in the Drawing-room."

"Tidy your hair, Miss Syringa," Nana said in an agitated

manner, taking off her apron, as she spoke. "Sit down and receive His Lordship like a lady. 'Tis important, very important that he should realise who you are!"

"And who am I?" Syringa asked.

However, obeying Nana, she ran across the hall and went into the Drawing-room which overlooked the lawn at the back of the house.

It was a pretty room and her mother had decorated it charmingly.

The furniture might not be of great value, the mirrors and pictures of no consequence, but the room reflected the taste of a Lady of Quality.

There was no mistaking the elegance of the sofa and chairs, even if they were threadbare, the soft blue damask hangings with cushions to match, and the mellow colours of the rug in front of the fireplace.

Syringa looked around her quickly.

Everything was neat and dusted, and she was glad that only yesterday she had put large vases of syringa on the tables on either side of the fireplace and a big bunch of daffodils in the window.

The whole room was fragrant with the scent of syringa. It came not only from the vases, but the casement windows were open and for the last few days the bushes in the garden had been a riot of white blossom.

Content with the room, Syringa glanced at herself in the mirror and tried to pat her hair into place.

It framed her cheeks in tiny curls and she realised that quite by accident, because her hair was thick and grew back from her forehead, she emulated the Ladies of Fashion with their hedgehog coiffeurs.

Her fichu was clean and crisp. Nana ironed one for her every day and, if her gown was old, its full skirts were spotlessly clean.

The sash with which she had encircled her waist made it look very small.

It was impossible for her to buy mourning to wear because she had no money. But she had fortunately found a mauve sash amongst her mother's belongings.

Otherwise she was all in white and her face was very pale as she listened to voices in the hall and then footsteps coming towards the door.

"The Earl of Rothingham, Miss Syringa," Nana answered.

The Earl entered the room to see a very pale, frightened little face turned towards him and two large grey eyes which were worried and apprehensive.

Then at the sight of him they changed.

A sudden sparkle seemed to light them up and a faint colour rose in her pale cheeks.

It was almost like seeing dawn come swiftly over the Indian plains, he thought.

Then Syringa said with a lilt in her voice.

"It was you! I was sure it must be! I am so glad!"

"Who else did you think it might be?" the Earl asked.

She had remembered him as being very tall and broad-shouldered, but now he seemed enormous in the small room. He also appeared so sophisticated and smartly dressed with his high cravat and well fitting coat that she felt small and insignificant and very shy.

He was waiting, she realised, for the answer to his question, but his expression was one of boredom.

"I had no idea," Syringa replied. "Then I thought that perhaps out of kindness you meant to buy Mercury! You saved him . . . you really did save him . . . from a horrible man. A man who I am convinced would have been cruel to him!"

"If that is the case, I am glad that I bought Mercury," the Earl said.

As if his words reminded Syringa that Mercury was not the only thing he had bought, she flushed and said quickly:

"I am forgetting my manners . . . would Your Lordship not sit down?"

"I wondered if you would ask me to do so," the Earl replied.

"I ... I am sorry," Syringa said. "You must forgive m-me, but I have been so anxious ... so worried."

She paused, and as the Earl stood looking at her she added:

"I am ... afraid I also ... forgot to ... curtsey."

The Earl walked to the arm-chair by the fireplace and sat down.

"I think we have quite a lot to discuss, Miss Melton."

Syringa sat opposite him on the edge of her chair and putting her hands in her lap she looked rather like a nervous child.

The Earl did not speak and after a moment she asked:

"Why did ... you do ... it?"

"Send my agent to bid at the Sale?" the Earl asked, making no pretence of not understanding her question. "I suppose I could tell you it was out of kindness because I was sorry for you, but that would not be entirely the truth."

Syringa's eyes widened, but she did not speak, and after a moment the Earl continued:

"I was sorry for you, but until I went back to King's Keep I thought your problems were no concern of mine."

"What changed your mind?" Syringa asked.

"I was looking at a map of the Estates," the Earl replied, "and I realised that while I owned the whole of the village of Whitley, the Manor House was not in my possession."

"My father bought it from yours," Syringa explained, "when he first married Mama."

"That is what I was told," the Earl said. "My father sold quite a number of pieces of property which were really not his to sell. But he took the money and there was nothing the Trustees could do except later try to repair the damage by buying them back."

"I can understand your wanting the Manor," Syringa murmured.

"I think you are really asking yourself why you were included in my purchases," the Earl remarked.

He seemed to drawl out the words deliberately and the

blood rushed into Syringa's cheeks and her eyes fell shyly before his.

"I can assure you," he added, "that it was quite by mistake."

"That is what I ... thought it ... must be," Syringa said breathlessly.

"I was, of course, unaware that your father would include you amongst his other possessions," the Earl explained. "I merely told my Agent to buy whatever was for sale and top the price of any other bidder."

"Why did you do that?" Syringa asked. "You could not have wanted the contents of the house."

"I thought perhaps I might let it furnished," the Earl replied, "in fact I imagined that you and your father would be glad to stay on as my tenants."

"That was kind of you ... very kind," Syringa murmured.

"But as I have said," the Earl continued, "I was personally interested in acquiring the property. It appeared to me to be a blot on the estate map, outlined in a different colour, so that I could not fail to notice it."

"In fact it was Naboth's vineyard!" Syringa smiled.

For the first time since he had entered the room there was a twinkle in the Earl's eyes.

"And the manner in which I had to obtain it was almost as dramatic."

"I am sorry ... I have proved so ... expensive," Syringa said, and now again her cheeks were flushed with colour. "I have been worrying, My Lord, as to how I could possibly repay you."

"Do you wish to do so?" the Earl enquired.

"But of course!" Syringa replied positively, "unfortunately ten thousand pounds is a terrible amount of money! I was saying to Nana – my old Nurse – that even if I worked all my life, I could never earn enough money to pay you back what you have expended."

"I think the best thing I can do," the Earl replied, "is to

wipe it off as a bad debt. No, that sounds rather rude! I should say a good debt."

Syringa twisted her hands together.

"My Lord, there is ... something I have to ... tell you," she said in a very small voice.

The Earl's eye-lids seemed to drop lazily over his eyes.

"And what could that be?" he asked, and now there was a mocking note in his voice. "Perhaps I can guess."

"How could you?" Syringa enquired.

"When beautiful young women say they wish to tell me something," the Earl replied, "it invariably involves a confession concerning matters of the heart. Who is the fortunate man of whom you wish to speak?"

"It is not like that," Syringa cried, "there is no ... man."

"No man?" the Earl questioned. "That I can hardly believe! You must have had many beaux. Even in such a quiet spot as this you have neighbours, Syringa, and if they are men they will have eyes and you will not have gone unnoticed."

"I am afraid, My Lord, you have entirely the wrong impression," Syringa said with an effort at dignity. "Mama did not wish to go into society. Although my father hunted and had some friends in the Country, Mama and I stayed at home."

"Why did your mother not wish to associate with other people?" the Earl asked.

"I think the ... real reason," Syringa answered hesitatingly, the colour rising in her cheeks, "was that we could not ... afford it. There was not enough money for Papa to be well dressed and well mounted and for ... us to be ... smartly gowned."

She paused then went on quickly :

"You must not think Mama minded. She much preferred being quietly at home, and when Papa was with her they were so happy they wanted no-one else. I think too, that Mama would not have accepted hospitality unless she could return it. And that was ... impossible."

"So you are really telling me the truth when you say you have no beaux," the Earl said.

"I always tell the truth, My Lord."

There was a note of defiance in the young voice.

"It seems incredible," the Earl remarked, "but perhaps you will forgive me for my suspicions and tell me what you wished to say."

Syringa was silent for a moment until the Earl said:

"It seems there is some difficulty! Are you afraid to confide in me?"

"Not afraid," Syringa answered, "it is just, My Lord, that I would not have you think that I was anything but strictly ... honest."

The Earl raised his eyebrows.

"I loved my father," Syringa began. "It was only after my mother died and he could not face life without her that he returned to the ... excesses in which he had ... indulged as a ... young man."

She drew a deep breath.

"Whilst Mama was alive, we were never in debt. What we could not afford ... we did not have. It was as ... easy as that."

"I understand that all your father's debts were paid," the Earl answered. "My Agent told me that his creditors went away satisfied and his gambling debts were met."

"That is true," Syringa answered, "and I am deeply grateful to you, My Lord, for enabling me to hold my head up and not to feel ashamed and humiliated by that great accumulation of debts which was quite ... terrifying."

"And what is worrying you now?" the Earl asked and his tone was kinder.

"It is just ... My Lord, that when my father ... died we had no ... money ... Nana and I. So I am ... afraid there is now ... something ... owing locally. Not much," she added, "but there was ... nothing left ... in the garden and Nana is ... old."

86

"Are you telling me," the Earl said, "that you and your Nurse have gone hungry?"

"I felt sure it would not be for long," Syringa replied, her eyes pleading with him to understand. "But I knew that we ought not to run up ... debts of any sort until we had seen ... you and explained the ... position. But you never ... came! So I was going to ride over to King's Keep this ... afternoon to ask when ... you would be there again."

"You have been hungry," the Earl said, almost as if he spoke to himself. "I thought you looked thinner."

"It does not matter about me," Syringa said hastily, "but there is Nana and ... Mercury."

"We must not forget Mercury!"

"To much young grass is not ... good for him," Syringa said, and again she was pleading with him to understand.

"I cannot believe it possible that I should have forgotten in so short a time that men and women without money cannot eat," the Earl said hoarsely, but it was as if he spoke to himself.

He rose to his feet as he spoke and Syringa rose too.

"Stay here," he said and walking from the room shut the door behind him.

She stared after him in perplexity, and then although the door was closed she could hear voices in the distance and realised that the Earl was speaking to Nurse in the kitchen.

She had a sudden fear that Nana would say too much.

How often had she re-iterated in the last week that she would like to give the Earl a piece of her mind.

"It is not his fault," Syringa had excused him. "Why should he worry about us? He did not intend to buy me, that was a mistake. How could he possibly wish to spend ten thousand pounds on a woman?"

Now she repeated the sum almost under her breath as she had said it a thousand times already.

It seemed to be written in lines of fire as she had lain awake in the darkness thinking over what had happened at the Sale. And then there had always been at the back of her mind a fear as to what kind of man the Earl of Rothingham might be.

But that was over. The Earl was not a stranger but her friend. The friend who had helped her in the wood, who had loved a dog called Judith and lost her. He was also Jupiter the god of the sky.

"I am no longer afraid," Syringa thought.

It seemed to her that the sunshine in the garden was more golden than it had been before.

It was some time before the Earl came back into the room. Syringa had been sitting in the window-seat.

She rose to her feet almost apprehensively, her eyes searching his face in case Nana had annoyed him.

He appeared unperturbed as he said:

"I have made arrangements for your immediate future, Syringa."

"What are they, My Lord?"

"I am taking you and your Nurse to stay at King's Keep."

"Taking us away from here?"

"Yes," he answered, "it would be impossible for you to stay here alone."

"Why?" Syringa asked in surprise.

The Earl seemed about to reply and then changed his mind.

"You will be more comfortable at King's Keep," he said "and certainly better fed!"

"Nana did not say too much, did she?" Syringa enquired. "She is very outspoken."

The Earl's eyes twinkled.

"I rather felt I was back in the nursery again."

"Oh, I am sorry," Syringa said quickly.

"There is no reason to be," the Earl answered. "As usual your Nurse was in the right. Nurses always are. But I was rather apprehensive that I might be stood in the corner and only given bread and water for supper!"

Syringa looked worried and he added:

"I am forgiven and she has started to pack. I am taking you now with me in my Phaeton."

Syringa's eyes gleamed with excitement and the Earl noticed how the sunshine picked out the flecks of gold in them.

"And Mercury?" she asked.

"I thought if you and I can manage alone, my groom could ride Mercury. There will be all the oats he wants waiting for him at King's Keep."

"Oh, thank you, thank you!" Syringa cried, "I was so worried about him."

"And not about yourself?" the Earl enquired.

"At times ... I felt rather ... empty inside," Syringa smiled.

He looked down at her.

"I shall have to fatten you up."

She looked up into his eyes and he added sharply:

"You absurd child! Can you not realise that honesty or pride or whatever you like to call it can be carried too far?"

"You have been listening to Nana," she said accusingly. "I did not want my ... owner to think that I was trying to get ... things out of ... him before he even ... knew me."

"Things!" the Earl exclaimed. "You talk as if a few eggs, some milk and a loaf of bread were diamonds."

"They would certainly have been more palatable," Syringa replied.

The Earl laughed.

"Come along," he said, "get your hat. We will go back to King's Keep and you shall enjoy the largest feast my Chef can provide."

"And the ... money we ... owe," Syringa asked in a small voice.

"Still worrying about it?" the Earl enquired. "Set your mind at rest, I have already given your Nurse all she has expended. She will pay the shops when the carriage comes to fetch her and your luggage."

"Oh, thank you!" Syringa cried again.

"Does it really mean so much to you?" the Earl asked in a wondering voice.

"I will never ... never in the whole of my life owe anybody ... one penny. I will never buy ... anything that I cannot ... afford. I will never ... never ... get into ... debt."

She spoke passionately, and then, as if she suddenly remembered, her fingers went up to her lips.

"But of course," she said in a low voice, "I will always be in ... debt to ... you."

"I have told you to forget it," the Earl said sharply. "If there is one thing I dislike, Syringa, it is women who whine on about a subject I have no wish to discuss."

His tone was authoritative and Syringa looked at him a little apprehensively.

There was something about him she thought which could be very frightening. He had been so friendly, so gentle and so understanding when she had met him in the wood. But now he was different.

It almost seemed as though there was a barrier between them, a barrier, she thought, which appeared to make him hard and almost aggressive towards her.

"I will get my hat," she said shyly, and dropping the Earl a little curtsey she went from the room.

She sped up to her bed-room where Nana was already on her knees in front of a round-topped trunk.

"Nana! Nana!" Syringa exclaimed excitedly, "we are to go to King's Keep!"

"I know," her Nurse answered, "His Lordship has told me. I don't know what your mother would have thought about it! I don't for sure."

"Why should Mama mind?" Syringa asked in surprise. "His Lordship says we cannot stay here alone, although why not I do not understand."

"This is His Lordship's house now, Miss Syringa, you must realise that. People would talk. You living here entirely alone except for me."

"Who would talk and who would care?" Syringa asked with a little shrug of her shoulders, "But it will be wonderful to be at King's Keep. You know how beautiful it is, Nana, and you know how fond I have always been of it."

"Yes, dearie," her Nurse replied.

Syringa felt that something was worrying her, but she could not imagine what it could be.

"Pack everything I have," Syringa said, "and, Nana, do not forget your iron. I shall look sadly unfashionable in the elegance and grandeur of His Lordship's home. But at least I can have fresh fichus and you can press my sashes into a good shape."

"We can't stay there long, Miss Syringa," Nurse murmured.

Syringa was intent on putting a large straw hat on her head and tying the ribbons under her chin.

"It is too hot for me to wear a cape," she said, "and anyway it is too threadbare. I will carry a shawl over my arm. Do I look all right?"

She turned towards her Nurse, her eyes shining. She looked very lovely, very young and very innocent.

"You look all right, dearie," Nana said and there was a suspicion of a sob in her voice.

"Cheer up, Nana," Syringa smiled. "I know you must mind leaving here, but think how wonderful it will be to have lots to eat and cups and cups and cups of tea for you!"

Her Nurse did not reply. Syringa pulled open the door and ran downstairs.

The Earl was already in the Phaeton, his horses were moving restlessly, eager to be off. The groom assisted Syringa up beside him and covered her knee with a light rug.

"Bring Mercury along at once, Jim," the Earl said to the groom, "and do not ride him hard. He is not up to scratch at the moment."

"Very good, M'Lord."

The Earl started his horses. Syringa looking up at him

knew she had never seen a man look so elegant or in charge of such magnificent horseflesh.

It was a thrill that she had never experienced before to be behind such fine animals.

She did not speak and after they were clear of the ill-kept drive and on to the highway the Earl asked:

"Are you all right?"

"I am very excited!" Syringa answered. "I suppose it is very reprehensible of me, but I do not mind leaving my home. It has not been a very happy place these past three years."

She was silent for a moment and then she added:

"But Nana seems upset that we are going to King's Keep. I cannot think why."

"Perhaps she is afraid of the big bad Earl."

Syringa laughed.

"I suppose that is the truth! Someone told her you were a Rake and I believe she is really shocked."

"Do you know what a Rake means?" the Earl replied.

Syringa considered for a moment.

"I think it means a man who is very gay and enjoys every moment of his life without worrying how other people may be affected. I suppose Charles II was a Rake and most of his courtiers."

The Earl laughed.

"I see you are well read, Miss Melton."

"I had lessons with the Vicar," Syringa explained. "Mama insisted that I should be well taught."

"I cannot believe the Vicar allowed you to read much about the Court of Charles II."

"My knowledge of such things certainly did not come from the Vicar," Syringa agreed. "But the Colonel allowed me to visit the Library at King's Keep ... your Library. I cannot tell you how much I am looking forward to seeing it again."

"I suspect you know my house better than I know it myself," the Earl said.

"I used to go there a great deal until the Colonel became really ill, and then he was allowed no visitors," Syringa replied. "I was very fond of him and he was most kind to me. He allowed me to ride in the woods.

"He permitted me to read his books and he taught me many things about the pictures, the furniture and your very magnificent silver."

"Now you in turn must tell me all about my possessions," the Earl suggested.

"I should like to do that," Syringa answered.

They drove a little further and then the Earl asked:

"Have you no relations?"

Syringa shook her head.

"Papa was an orphan and my mother's father and mother never spoke to her after she ran away with Papa. My grandfather died, I believe, shortly after Mama, which was why the money that we used to live on came to an end."

"No aunts, cousins, relatives of any sort?" the Earl enquired.

"I am afraid not," Syringa said, "or if there are, I do not know of them."

She was silent for a moment and then she said in a very low voice:

"Are you frightened that I shall be an ... encumbrance? I promise you, My Lord, I will do my very best to think of some ... manner in which I can support myself."

"And have you any qualifications for such a formidable task?" the Earl asked.

"None, apart from being educated and being able to ride," Syringa answered. "Do you think perhaps I could break in horses? I am told that some women work in Livery Stables so that the Ladies of Quality can look elegant on horseback even if they are not good riders."

"That is certainly not a job I would recommend for you," the Earl said, and his tone was decisive.

"Well perhaps we will be able to think of something

93

soon," Syringa said. "I will not be a trouble, I promise you, and if you wish to be rid of me, you have only to shut me up in your Library."

The Earl seemed amused and at that moment they turned in through the huge gates of King's Keep.

Surmounted by two stone lions, which seemed to stand sentinel not only over the entrance but over the huge surrounding wall, the gates embellished with the Roth Coat-of-Arms were magnificent.

But they were only a prelude, Syringa thought, to the beauty of the avenue with its ancient oak trees, and the first sight of King's Keep itself standing out in its majesty in the valley between the green hills.

As always when she saw it, Syringa drew in her breath at the sheer beauty of the great stone building with its hundreds of iridescent windows and the shimmering silver of the lakes at its feet.

"It impresses you?" she heard the Earl ask.

"It is lovely!" Syringa answered. "Every time I see it, it seems more beautiful than the time before. I have not seen anything of the world, but I am sure that no palace in any other country could be more breath-taking."

"That is what I always think myself."

There was a note of sincerity in the Earl's voice which was unmistakable.

"You used to think about it when you were away, did you not?" Syringa asked.

"How did you know that?" he asked in surprise.

"I felt sure of it," she answered. "Even I, who have no bond with King's Keep, dream about it and, when I am very frightened or unhappy, the thought of it, solid, secure and safe all through the centuries, comforts me."

She knew the Earl agreed with her even though he did not say so, only tooling his horses with an expertise which aroused her admiration. He drew them to a standstill in front of the great front door with a flight of stone steps leading up to it.

Syringa was helped from the Phaeton, and then as the Earl joined her on the steps he held out his hand.

"Welcome to King's Keep!"

She smiled up at him, her eyes were like stars as she said breathlessly:

"It is so ... exciting being here with ... you."

# Chapter Five

Syringa was humming as she finished dressing.

"It is a lovely day, Nana," she said, "and there are so many thrilling things to do."

"You had a good night?" her Nurse asked.

"I fell asleep the moment my head touched the pillow," Syringa answered.

Nurse gave a sigh. It sounded like one of relief.

"Have a nice ride on Mercury, dearie," she said. "You look better already."

"And I feel fatter," Syringa laughed.

She thought of the large dinner that had been served last night and how exciting it had been to sit opposite the Earl in the small Dining-room which he used when he was alone.

There had been dish after dish of delicious and exotic food, but while at first Syringa had thought she was hungry, she soon found it impossible to eat any more.

The Earl had watched her with a smile as she regretfully declined the quails in aspic and a syllabub of lemon and cream.

"I promised you I would fatten you up," he complained, "but it seems unlikely if you refuse every dish that is offered to you."

"I have eaten so much already," Syringa said, "and it has all been so delicious! I had no idea that food could taste so good."

"Anything tastes good if you are hungry," the Earl smiled.

He told her a story how once, when he was in India, he

was lost for two days on the plains without food or water.

It seemed to Syringa they had been telling each other stories the whole afternoon.

They had made a tour of the house and she had related to him some of the interesting tales the Colonel had told her about the furniture, the pictures, and the exquisite Objets d'art which had been collected by the Roths down the centuries.

In a cabinet in the Blue Salon there was the watch set in crystal that Charles I had given on the scaffold to Sir Richard Roth.

Hanging in the Library was a portrait of his son Charles II, which had been painted when he stayed at King's Keep with the house in the background.

There was a walnut table which Queen Anne had presented to the Earl of Rothingham and the medals he had gained when fighting with Marlborough. And there was a portrait of the 1st Earl in his sleep painted by Moratti.

"I said you probably knew more about my house than I know myself," the Earl said when they had retired to the Green Salon for tea.

Syringa spooned the tea leaves from the silver canister which in the previous century had been kept locked because tea was so expensive, and poured from a beautiful silver teapot which had been given to the Earl of Rothingham in the reign of George I.

There had been cakes and sandwiches and tiny scones to eat, and having finished Syringa sat down on the hearth-rug at the Earl's feet.

It was a warm day, but there were fires in all the big rooms which, having not been lived in for so long, struck chilly when one first entered them.

"You look happy," the Earl said after a moment.

"I am happy!" Syringa replied, "happier than I ever remember being before. Perhaps it is the contrast from being so miserable for so long."

He did not answer; only his eyes watched her, noting the

soft curve of her lips and the clear line of her pointed chin above her long white neck. They talked about the house until it was time to dress for dinner.

"Do you realise," Syringa asked when she joined the Earl in one of the big Ante-rooms filled with pictures of his ancestors, "that this is the first time I have ever dined alone with a man?"

"I am honoured," the Earl replied.

"I am only telling you that in case I make mistakes or worse still you find me a bore," Syringa said frankly. "But there are so many things I wish to talk about to Your Lordship. I can only ask you to forgive me if you find it wearying."

"I am not likely to do that," the Earl replied in his deep voice.

Syringa had made him laugh during dinner and their conversation flowed without a pause until they retired to the Library.

"I thought we would sit here this evening," the Earl said.

He looked round the magnificent book-lined room with its long high windows covered with red velvet curtains, a huge desk in the centre of a fine Persian carpet, and the big comfortable sofas set in front of the log fire.

"I love this room," Syringa said. "Whenever I have come here I have always felt as though I was entering a treasure-house full of secrets more valuable and more precious than any jewels."

The Earl smiled.

"You must tell me what you have enjoyed reading," he said.

"I like best the books about Charles II," Syringa answered. "There are so many here because the King hid at King's Keep. I love to think of him coming back to England after all those years of exile. Then England became joyful and gay again and the King the gayest of all!"

She stopped speaking and clasped her hands together.

"I have just remembered something so exciting I found in

a book in the Library!" she cried. "Did you know that your name Ancelin means 'a god'?"

"Yes, I was aware of it," the Earl replied.

"Is it not a strange coincidence," Syringa went on, "that the moment I saw you you reminded me of Jupiter?"

"Very strange!" the Earl agreed.

They talked for a little longer about books, until the Earl realised that Syringa's eyelids were dropping and her replies to his questions were getting slower and slightly incoherent.

"You are tired," he said suddenly. "Go to bed, child. I should have remembered that you would be weak after eating so little for so long."

"I do feel sleepy," Syringa admitted.

She rose to her feet and standing beside his chair she said softly:

"Thank you ... thank you ... for a wonderful day. I hate to think it is over, but ... there is always tomorrow ... is there not?"

"Yes, there is always tomorrow," the Earl agreed.

She curtsied, and before he could rise to open the door for her, she had slipped away from the room.

Upstairs Nana was waiting for her in the Big State Bedroom with its huge four-poster bed, hung with embroidered curtains.

"Oh, Nana, why did you wait up?" Syringa asked. "You know I always put myself to bed!"

"I wanted to see you safe and sound," her Nurse answered.

She hesitated a moment and asked:

"You wouldn't like me to sleep with you, Miss Syringa?"

"Sleep with me!" Syringa exclaimed in astonishment. "Why, Nana, what a ridiculous idea!"

"I don't like leaving you alone," the Nurse said.

"I have always been alone," Syringa answered.

"Then promise me, dearie, that you will lock your door."

"But why? Why should I do that?" Syringa enquired.

Her Nurse seemed about to speak, and then obviously changed the words she was about to say.

"There is talk of robbers in the neighbourhood," she murmured.

"Robbers!"

Syringa laughed.

"I do not believe it, and even if there are they would find it hard to get into King's Keep. His Lordship was telling me this afternoon that he has appointed two new Night Watchmen. So you can sleep comfortably in your bed, Nana, without worrying."

"Lock your door, Miss Syringa, I beg of you," Nurse pleaded.

"All right, if it gives you any pleasure," Syringa agreed yawning. "I am too tired to argue."

She slipped her nightgown over her head and heard Nana move towards the door before she said insistently:

"Say your prayers and then lock the door."

"Very well," Syringa agreed, "and good night, Nana dear. Do stop worrying about me."

Her Nurse shut the door and Syringa was alone.

What could be agitating the old woman? she wondered. It was so unlike Nana to fuss. Who could possible harm her at King's Keep?

She was so tired that she slipped straight into bed.

"I will say my prayers lying down," she thought.

Then, almost before she had finished the first one, she was asleep.

Awaking after a long dreamless night, she felt all the exuberance and vitality of youth rushing back into her body again.

It was a wonderful change after the listlessness and apathy she had felt this past week when there had been insufficient to eat.

The breakfast that Nana had brought her was delicious, and she knew that she was ready for a long gallop on Mercury. He too, she thought, would be very much more frisky than he had been without his oats.

"Goodbye, Nana," she said.

She picked up her gloves and riding-whip and went from the bed-room to the top of the Grand Staircase.

She heard voices, and as she descended the staircase slowly savouring the softness of the thick pile carpet under her feet and the splendour of the huge portraits by Van Dyke on the walls, she saw three men waiting below in the Hall.

One of them was speaking to Barnham the butler, when she heard him saying:

"His Lordship is just finishing breakfast. I've sent a foot-man to inform him you're here."

Even as he spoke Syringa heard the Earl's voice ask:

"What is all this about?"

He came into the Hall and she saw he was wearing riding breeches and a cut-away blue coat. His white cravat meticulously and intricately tied looked very white against the dark panelling.

"We've caught a poacher in th' very act, My Lord," one of them said. "He'd a snare in one hand and a rabbit in th' other. As I say to him, ''Tis transportation for ye, m' man'."

"What is his explanation?" the Earl asked.

"He ain't said nothin', M'Lord. Seems a bit simple like, but that's no excuse. Some of these here poachers be clever enough to keep their mouths shut so as not to incriminate 'emselves."

It was not easy for Syringa to see the man who was accused as he was standing between two keepers, but now as she nearly reached the Hall she heard the Earl say sharply:

"What have you got to say for yourself, man? This is your only chance, before I send you to the magistrates."

There was no answer, and after a moment the Earl said:

"Very well. Take him away and have him charged."

The keepers turned to obey. Then as Syringa reached the

Hall she saw who it was between them. She moved forward with a little cry.

"Stop! Stop! There is some mistake!"

"There is no mistake," the Earl said, "and this does not concern you, Syringa."

"It does concern me!" Syringa retorted. "This man is not a poacher. He is old Ben and I know him well, he lives in the woods."

"I found him with a snare in his hand, Ma'am," one of the keepers said, holding up a contraption of wood and string, "and there be th' rabbit."

He pointed to the dead rabbit which the other keeper held in his hand.

"'Twere alive when we found it," the man went on, "but it died on th' way here."

"He was setting it free ... of course he was setting it free!" Syringa cried. "Ben would never harm a wild animal."

"It is no use trying to defend the man," the Earl said. "My keepers have caught him in the act and you know as well as I do that poaching is a crime that cannot be tolerated. If he had anything to say in his defence, he would have said it by now."

Syringa turned to face the Earl, her eyes wide and troubled.

"Ben never speaks, I think he was born dumb. He hums little tunes to the birds and to the animals who trust him, and he makes himself understood to other people by signs. He would never have killed that rabbit, I know that."

"I am sorry, Syringa," the Earl said. "My keepers must do their duty, and I must support them while they are doing it."

Syringa looked up at him pleadingly and it seemed to her as if he avoided her eyes. She knew then that he was determined to ignore anything she might say.

The keepers, as if they felt the conversation was at an end, took Ben by the arm and turned him towards the door.

They had only taken a few steps when Syringa's voice rang out.

"Stop! Wait! I will prove what I say!"

The two men looked at the Earl as if waiting his orders but he remained silent and Syringa said:

"Please stand on one side."

Then she said quietly to the old man:

"Listen, Ben, I want to help you."

His face was deeply lined and his hair was white, but there was something almost puckish in his old face and there was a faint smile on his lips as he looked at her.

He wore a ragged old coat with big patch pockets over a tattered waistcoat. His boots were tied up with string and there was a dirty cotton handkerchief round his neck.

Syringa standing facing him, her eyes on his, said:

"Ben, show His Lordship what you have in your pocket."

The old man glanced over his shoulder as if to see the keepers were not too near and then from the pocket on his right hand side he drew out a small red squirrel.

He held it in his hands, then it ran up his arm and sat on his shoulder. He gave it a nut and the squirrel cracked it between his teeth, his little eyes glancing round curiously as he did so.

"And now in your other pocket," Syringa said, her voice very low, hardly above a whisper.

Ben put his big hand into his pocket and drew out three small field-mice.

They ran up his other arm and peeped round his collar. Then seeing the squirrel they scuttled back for safety into the warm pocket.

"And what else have you to show His Lordship?" Syringa prompted.

He put his hand inside his coat and produced a young wood-pigeon.

He held it gently in his big hands and they could all see that one of the bird's legs was strapped with a small sliver of stick. It was skilfully bound.

Old Ben caressed the grey feathers with one of his fingers and the pigeon sat quite still, its small bright eyes unafraid.

"Have you anything else?" Syringa asked.

The old man shook his head. Syringa turned towards the Earl.

"Do you think," she asked, "that if there was blood on his hands these animals would trust him?"

There was silence for a moment and then the Earl said:

"You have proved your point – the man goes free."

"But My Lord!" one of the keepers expostulated, "if he is allowed to wander over the woods in the nesting season he will disturb the pheasants, and we were looking forward to providing good shooting for Your Lordship in the autumn."

"Shooting!"

Syringa suddenly went pale.

It was as if she realised what was meant by keepers patrolling the woods. If later in the year they were beaten out, what would become of the Secret Place?

Without realising she was doing so she laid her hand on the Earl's arm. He understood what she meant.

"I have given orders already," he said, "that Monks Wood is to be a sanctuary. The keepers will not go there."

Syringa gave a quick sigh of relief and turned to tell Ben where he would be safe. But the old man had left.

He had slipped away as silently and as quickly as he moved through the woods and had gone back to the world he knew. The world of birds and animals, creatures who were injured and in pain and who trusted him.

It was when the Earl and Syringa were riding across the Park, their horses skittish from sheer exuberance, that Syringa managed to say:

"Thank you for releasing Ben. I knew you would understand."

"I am glad you prevented me from making a mistake," the Earl said.

"Must you employ keepers on the Estate?" she asked. "It

has been so quiet and peaceful in the woods until now."

"They are unfortunately full of vermin," the Earl replied, "and vermin can be as cruel as human beings if they are allowed to get out of hand."

"I understand that," Syringa said, "but at the same time I have loved the wildness of the woods, the feeling that everything is free and untroubled."

"I would wish my lands to be a model of their kind," the Earl replied.

She knew by the tone in his voice that he was determined to make improvements and that nothing she could say would alter his decision.

Their ride was an enjoyable one, and when they turned for home Syringa's cheeks were flushed and she seemed to glow not only from the exercise, but from happiness.

Her habit was very old and almost threadbare. But the dark blue velvet accentuated the whiteness of her skin, and the little three-cornered hat set on her hair seemed to give it a colour that the Earl had not noticed before.

She rode extremely well, an instinctive rider with soft hands, yet who could make a horse obey her.

"I must have many more horses in the stable," the Earl said aloud. "I plan to enlarge the place and soon you will have a big choice of mounts, Syringa."

"I never want one that is better than Mercury," Syringa replied, "and I doubt if you could find one."

"You are offering me a challenge," the Earl said with a smile. "But I grant you that Mercury is a very fine piece of horseflesh."

"You know that the Colonel gave him to me."

"I had no idea," the Earl replied.

"He was bred here at King's Keep," Syringa said. "When he was a foal the Colonel thought he had too many horses, so he gave me a choice of Mercury and four others."

"You chose the right one!"

"I know I did," Syringa replied. "You do see that Mercury has come home?"

"I see in one way or another," the Earl remarked, "that you are indivisibly linked with King's Keep."

"I like to think so," Syringa answered, looking at the great house ahead of them, the sunshine glinting on its windows, the white swans moving slowly and majestically across the lake.

In the weeks the Earl had been away, the garden had burst into bloom, the white cherry and pink almond trees had a fairy like quality, and the purple lilac and its pale sister intermingled with the bushes of fragrant syringa.

It was so beautiful that even Syringa, who had known the gardens for so many years, felt it lovelier than she had ever known it before.

Then she told herself it was only because she was so happy.

When they reached the house, the grooms took away the horses and Syringa went upstairs to change her riding habit.

When she came downstairs again she was surprised to hear a number of people talking outside the front door.

She looked with a question in her eyes at Barnham, who said:

"It's them Italians, Miss, from the west side of the Estate. They're waiting to see His Lordship."

"Italians!" Syringa cried. "Oh, I must speak to them!"

She went out through the front door and saw grouped at the bottom of the steps twenty or more people, mostly men.

"Why it's Miss Syringa Melton!" an old man exclaimed in surprise, his words tinged with an accent.

"Signor Giulio. How are you? But why are you here? I thought you never travelled far from your house and your workshop."

"We've had terrible news, Signorina!" the old man answered, "terrible news indeed!"

"Why, what has happened?" Syringa enquired.

"We've been told to leave, Miss Syringa, leave our homes and clear out!"

"Who could have told you to do such a thing?" Syringa

gasped, with a sudden fear in her heart.

She had known the Italians who lived on the Estate ever since she had been a child. There was a small colony of them in the houses they had occupied when they had first come to England.

Many of the older men had died, but those who remained had multiplied, and Syringa reckoned now they must be a community of forty or fifty having little social contact with people in the nearby villages, but managing to exist on local employment.

That they should be sent away after so many years seemed incredible and Syringa waited apprehensively for the answer to her question.

"'Tis Mister Hempster, Miss Syringa. He's never liked us and he's ordered us to go at once. But where, I ask the Signorina, where?"

"Has he His Lordship's authority for giving you notice?" Syringa enquired.

"How should we know, Miss Syringa? I understands Mister Hempster is with His Lordship at this moment. He is our enemy – a cruel relentless enemy, Miss Syringa, as you know."

"Yes, indeed I know," Syringa replied.

She looked round at the men's faces listening to what was being said and saw the desperate anxiety in their eloquent dark eyes.

"I will see what I can do," she said and turning ran up the steps again.

"Where is His Lordship?" she asked Barnham.

"He is with Mr. Hempster, Miss, in the Writing Room."

Syringa knew this was rather an austere and formal room where the Colonel had dealt with the Estate matters when he was too old to go to the Office.

She moved quickly down the passage, hesitated a moment outside the door, then opened it and went in.

The Earl was sitting at the desk and in front of him was Mr. Hempster.

He was a man of about fifty with a red face and hard beady eyes set too close together. Syringa had never liked him and there were many local stories about his being a bully and at times over harsh with his horses.

The Earl looked up impatiently at her entrance.

"I am busy, Syringa."

"I am here, My Lord, as . . . Counsel for the Defence."

She saw a quickly repressed twinkle in the Earl's eye before he said sharply:

"This is an Estate matter and I wish to deal with it in my own way."

"At least, My Lord, hear what these people have to say on their own behalf," Syringa pleaded. "Or let me say it for them."

Before the Earl could speak, Mr. Hempster said almost aggressively:

"Miss Melton can know nothing of this problem, M'Lord."

His words made the Earl change his mind.

"That is for me to judge, Hempster," he replied coldly. "Well, Syringa, what have you to tell me?"

"I do not know whether you are aware, My Lord," Syringa replied, "that the Italians were brought here originally by your grandfather. It was they who built his Observatory on the hill, who painted and gilded the ceiling of the house."

She looked up before she went on:

"They worked under the great masters who came from Italy to decorate the Banqueting Hall and the Salons and carried out the designs of Bagutte and Plura for the chimney pieces. There were of course originally more of them, and although a number returned home some remained."

She paused and looking at Mr. Hempster said:

"They are hard working decent people, but they have inadvertently incurred the enmity of your Farm Bailiff. He has always tried to get rid of them. The Colonel refused to listen to him, and now he hopes to succeed with Your Lordship, where he has failed before."

"And why did the Colonel refuse such a request?" the Earl asked.

"Because, My Lord, he was too old to realise what was going on," the Bailiff interposed angrily before Syringa could speak. "He didn't realise he was being diddled by these lazy lay-abouts, these dirty foreigners who have no right on our land."

"And what is your explanation?" the Earl asked turning to Syringa.

"The Colonel recognised what value they were to the Estate," Syringa answered. "Who do you think has mended the furniture in this house, who has painted the walls, who has done the small repairs which are needed week after week all the year round? These men are craftsmen, skilful and artistic, and can be trusted with your most valuable possessions."

"The work can be done just as well by the English carpenters," Mr. Hempster said angrily.

"What is more," Syringa continued ignoring the interruption, her eyes on the Earl, "after they have been here so long, they are your people! They belong to King's Keep as much as anyone else on the Estate. Although they are of Italian origin, they have chosen to stay here in England and their children born in this country are English."

She paused then raised her voice a little.

"Why should they be sent away for no reason except that Mr. Hempster hates them?"

"Is this true?" the Earl asked turning to his Bailiff. "Do you hate them?"

"I know them for what they are, M'Lord, a lot of ne'er-do-wells, thieving, poaching, defiling the land. They're no good. If your Lordship takes my advice, you'll be rid of them. I've told them to go and I only wants Your Lordship to support me as I hope Your Lordship will in other things."

The Earl seemed to consider for a moment and then Syringa said:

"I cannot think that it is just to allow a personal prejudice to affect the lives of so many people who have served King's Keep well and to the best of their ability."

"A personal prejudice?" the Earl asked sharply.

"Five years ago," Syringa answered, "Mr. Hempster's daughter ran away with one of the Italians. He has never forgiven her or Antonio's relatives."

"Is this true?" the Earl asked of his Bailiff.

The man was glaring at Syringa and it was obvious that his temper was rising fast.

"Yes, M'Lord, 'tis true. Women – all women – are besotted by their soft tongues and their dark eyes. They go lusting after those slimy devils and lose all sense of decency."

"I will enquire further into your complaints," the Earl said coldly. "In the meantime the Italians will remain where they are and receive the consideration they have always had."

"So Your Lordship means to reverse my orders?" the Bailiff asked in an ugly voice.

It was obvious to Syringa he had lost his temper.

"Then all I can say is that Your Lordship is making a sad mistake which you will regret," he went on. "That's what comes of listening to foreigners and to – women! Why does Miss Melton meddle in such matters when she should have been trying to prevent her father drinking himself insensible?"

He glared at Syringa before he went on:

" 'Tis against your interests, M'Lord, to allow these scallywags to remain, whatever some fancy woman from the village may say."

He almost spat the words at Syringa as he spoke, and she took a step backwards in surprise.

"That is enough!" the Earl said rising to his feet. "I will have no-one in my employment speaking in such a manner to a lady! You will leave my service immediately and your house within a week."

He did not raise his voice but his words were like a whiplash. Mr. Hempster's anger evaporated and he cringed.

"I apologise, M'Lord. You can't mean what Your Lordship's just said."

"I mean it," the Earl replied.

He took Syringa by the arm as he spoke and drew her beside him through the door, leaving the Bailiff alone in the Writing Room.

They walked down the the passage and because she felt so relieved at his decision, she clung on to his arm, with both hands and laid her cheek against his shoulder.

"You were right! Right to dismiss him! He is a horrible man, he always has been. No-one would have told you, but he has earned the Estate a bad name for a long time."

They had reached the Hall, the Earl looked down at Syringa with a faint smile on his lips.

"Are you going to break the good news to my Italian tenants," he enquired, "or am I?"

"But you, of course!" she answered. "I want them to realise how kind, how just and how . . . wonderful you are."

Her voice was very soft, but the Earl seemed to listen to it. For a long moment he looked down into her eyes shining with admiration and joy.

Then he disengaged his arm from her hands and walked towards the front door.

That evening they had dined in the big Banqueting Hall with its fabulous pictures by Verrio on the walls and on the ceilings.

It was only as they sat down at the table which was decorated with flowers and seemed to Syringa to be weighed down with gold plate, that she glanced up at the ceiling and gave a little exclamation.

"What has surprised you?" the Earl said.

"Jupiter!" she replied. "Do you see that Verrio painted Jupiter in the centre of the ceiling? I never realised it before, and yet there he is surrounded by his goddesses in all his glory."

"And do you still find a resemblance to me?" the Earl asked a little dryly.

Syringa threw back her head revealing as she did so the rounded column of her white neck and the soft curves of her small breasts.

Her gown was very simple. It was old and had been made by Nana but it became her. Soft muslin framed her shoulders, a sash made her waist appear very small, and her full skirts billowed out attractively.

"Jupiter, as Verrio saw him, is very handsome," Syringa answered, "but not as handsome as you."

She turned her eyes as she spoke from the ceiling to the Earl and she thought, as he sat in his high-backed chair very much at his ease, that no-one could look more magnificent, or indeed more commanding.

"You flatter me," the Earl demurred.

"Is it flattery to speak the truth?" Syringa asked.

"If I told you that you were very beautiful," the Earl replied, "would you call that flattery?"

Syringa hesitated a moment and then a dimple appeared at the side of her mouth.

"I should make every effort to believe Your Lordship spoke the truth."

"Then of course I must believe you."

"I always think it so tiresome to be told one should not say nice things to people," Syringa said. "I remember once when I was with Mama, we met a lady with a little girl and Mama said:

'How very pretty your daughter is!'

And the lady replied:

'Hush, not in front of her, we go to a lot of trouble not to let her grow conceited'."

"And did you grow conceited at the nice things your mother said to you?" the Earl asked.

"I think Mama thought I was quite nice-looking," Syringa replied, "but she really only had eyes for Papa and he always said – 'if you are half as pretty as your mother when you grow up you will be very fortunate.'"

Her voice was a little wistful and the Earl said almost harshly.

"Now you are grown up, you will find plenty of men ready to pay you compliments, to praise the beauty of your eyes or write an ode to your eyebrows."

Syringa laughed.

"I am unlikely to meet such men. But if I do, I will merely tell them they are being nonsensical."

"You would not like a poem written to you?" the Earl asked.

"It would depend who wrote it," Syringa answered. "If you wrote one, for instance, I should ... treasure it always."

"You are quite safe," the Earl replied, "I do not write poetry and I would not insult you with bad verse."

"Perhaps you do not think me worthy of ... a poem," Syringa suggested, but it seemed as if he had not heard her.

After dinner they went again to the Library. Syringa sat down on the sofa and said:

"I shall not disgrace myself tonight by falling asleep. I thought as I undressed that you might think I had been rude. But it was difficult to keep my eyes open."

"You slept well?" the Earl asked.

"So well that I fell asleep while I was saying my prayers, and I never locked the door as Nana had asked me to do."

There was a moment's silence.

"Why did she ask you to do that?"

"I cannot imagine," Syringa replied. "She had some nonsensical story that there were robbers in the neighbourhood, but I have never heard of robbers trying to get into King's Keep. And when we lived at the Manor no-one came to rob us."

She gave a little laugh.

"I think Nana was just fussing over me to make herself important. I believe, although she likes being at King's Keep and enjoys the comfort, she rather misses the autocratic position she had at the Manor, when there was no-one to argue or prevent her from doing anything she wished."

They talked until after eleven o'clock.

Then Syringa saw the Earl glance at the clock on the mantelpiece and felt it was up to her to make the first move to go to bed.

"Perhaps I should retire," she suggested. "I do not want to keep you talking if you wish to read. Will we be riding again in the morning?"

"If it pleases you," the Earl replied.

"You know how much I enjoy it," she answered. "Shall we have a race tomorrow, although I am afraid Thunderer will easily outpace Mercury."

"I might give you a short start," the Earl conceded.

"Then that is what we will do," Syringa said. "I will be ready at nine o'clock."

She smiled at him then curtsied and said softly:

"Thank you ... Lord Jupiter, for another wonderful ... wonderful ... day. I have been so ... happy."

The Earl rose to his feet slowly, but already Syringa had reached the door. She turned to look back at him her eyes shining in her small face.

"It is a pity," she said, "that Verrio could not have seen you before he painted the scene in the Banqueting Hall."

Then the door shut behind her and the Earl stood looking at it as if he expected it to open again.

Syringa had been in bed for some time and was reading a book that she had taken from the Library earlier in the afternoon.

There was a candelabra holding three candles at her side and she had pulled the curtain of the four-poster back against the wall.

She heard the door open and for a moment did not look up, thinking it must be Nana returning for something she had forgotten.

She heard the door shut again, realised someone was in the room and turning her head saw the Earl.

He was wearing a long brocade robe with a high velvet collar above which the white frill of his night-shirt framed his chin. He looked extremely attractive and there was a buccaneering glint in his eyes.

Syringa threw down her book.

"You have come to say goodnight to me!" she exclaimed, and there was a note of joy in her voice. "How kind of you! I cannot tell you how much I miss Mama saying goodnight to me after I have got into bed."

The Earl came slowly across the room and when he reached Syringa's side he sat down on the bed facing her.

She looked small and very fragile against the big pillows with their frilled edges.

The candle light shone on her hair finding little strands of gold and the Earl saw that she was wearing a muslin night gown which buttoned at the neck, with a small flat collar edged with lace.

The sleeves were long and the lace-trimmed cuffs fell over her long thin fingers.

She looked very young, almost a child, and yet the muslin was thin and the soft curved outlines of her tip-tilted breasts were revealed by the candles.

"When I was small Mama used to tell me a story every night," Syringa went on, "but now I have to read one for myself. I like to go to sleep thinking of gallant deeds or beautiful places in the world which perhaps I will never be fortunate enough to see."

The Earl did not speak but was looking at her in what seemed to be a strange way. Because she sensed instinctively that something was disturbing him, Syringa said:

"I know that your mother died when you were only two. You must have missed her terribly without realising you were ... doing so."

"Perhaps I did," the Earl replied speaking for the first time.

"You have been through a lot of unhappiness," Syringa went on, "but now you will be happy. How can you help it when you are in your home at last?"

"Supposing I am lonely?" the Earl asked.

"How could you be?" she enquired. "You must have many friends and so much to do."

The Earl did not reply and after a moment she said:

"When I was saying my prayers tonight ... and I said them properly kneeling by the bed ... I thanked God because we had met. I thanked Him that you had bought Mercury and me."

The Earl made an impatient movement and Syringa said quickly.

"I know you told me not to talk about it, but I was so afraid that someone would buy Mercury and be cruel to him. Well I think the same applied to me. If anyone else had bid for me at that Sale ... they might have been ... cruel and ... frightening."

"You are not frightened of me?" the Earl asked.

It was as if a thousand candles lit Syringa's face.

"How could I be afraid of you?" she asked. "You are my friend, a friend I have wanted so badly, a friend I have never had before in my whole life."

"You wanted a friend?"

"I always thought how marvellous it would be to have one, someone to talk to, someone to laugh with, someone who would understand."

Syringa gave a little sigh.

"When I met you in the wood, it was everything I had ever hoped for. You were so wise, and yet so gentle and understanding. You made me see how foolish and cowardly I was being and when you left me ... nothing was quite so dark and frightening as it had been before."

Her grey eyes looked at him, as if he dazzled her.

They were wide and the Earl felt they were clear as a stream rippling over gravel. There was nothing hidden, nothing concealed!

"What do you know about love, Syringa?" he asked and there was a deep note in his voice.

Syringa made an eloquent gesture with her hands.

"I suppose the truth is that I know nothing," she answered. "I know how much in love Mama and Papa were with each other, but once Mama said to me – 'Never, Syringa, never give yourself to a man unless you love him.'"

Syringa's eyes look perplexed.

"I do not quite know what Mama meant by 'giving yourself to a man', but I suppose she was telling me not to marry anyone unless I loved him with all my heart."

The Earl was silent and Syringa went on :

"I would, of course, not think of marrying unless I was deeply in love. Perhaps no-one will ever ask me, but if someone did I would want to love him very, very much indeed."

"And if you were in love – what do you think you would feel?" the Earl asked.

Syringa considered for a moment, then she said shyly :

"I think the man ... I loved, if he ... loved me, would ... lift me up to the sky ... so that we would forget the world ... and be aware only of ... ourselves and our ... love."

Her voice died away into silence.

Then she asked :

"Is that why ... you have never married? Because you have never found anyone who you could love like ... that?"

"Yes – that is the reason."

"And yet there must have been lots of ladies who loved you," Syringa said reflectively. "When a man is attractive like ... you and Charles II, there must always be beautiful ladies who ... want your attention, who wish to steal your heart ... if they can do so."

"And as you have already pointed out," the Earl said with a twist to his lips. "Charles II was a Rake and so am I."

"Perhaps that is what makes you so attractive," Syringa replied. "I think women like men to be dashing, adventurous, and brave."

"And you think I am all those things?" the Earl enquired.

"Oh and much more!" Syringa cried. "You are wise and you are kind too! I would rather have you as a friend than anyone in the whole world."

"As a friend?" the Earl repeated.

There was silence and then Syringa said humbly:

"Perhaps you do not consider me clever enough to be your friend. I realise I am very ignorant and I know very little of the world. I have read lots of books but that is not the same, is it?"

He did not answer and she went on:

"And you have lived so fully and been to so many strange and interesting places. Perhaps I am just ... someone you could ... easily forget."

"I assure you I shall not do that," the Earl said.

"Are you sure?"

"Quite sure!"

"Then ... may I be your ... friend?" Syringa asked.

"And what do you think that implies?" the Earl asked, his eyes on hers.

"I am not quite ... certain," she answered, "but I think it means someone to whom I can tell my ... innermost secrets. Someone who will not think I am fanciful if I am ... apprehensive or ... worried. Someone with whom I can share not only the unhappy things in my life, but the happy ones. And most of all ... someone with whom I can ... laugh."

She hesitated a moment and then she added:

"I think that is really what makes me feel most lonely. It is not easy to laugh with one's parents, they are so much older. And Mercury, marvellous though he is ... does not really see a joke."

The Earl found himself laughing.

"I see we have a lot to offer each other," he said. "But you know, Syringa, that being a friend involves taking as well as giving."

"I know that," Syringa said, "and that is why I want you to give me your trust ... to let me ... help you if I ... can.

You know that I would always be ... loyal whatever ... happens."

"And what do you think might happen?" the Earl asked.

"I do not know," Syringa answered, "but I feel that something is ... puzzling you ... something you are not quite sure about and ... I want to ... help you."

She looked up at him as she spoke. Their eyes met in the candle-light and suddenly she had a very strange feeling.

She felt as if he was asking something and at the same time pulling her towards him.

That she was being swept along by a power over which she had no control, nearer and still nearer.

It was very hard to breathe, her lips were parted, then her hands made a little convulsive gesture and the spell was broken.

The Earl rose to his feet.

"Goodnight, Syringa," he said, "I will try to be your friend."

"Oh thank you, that means more to me than I can ever tell you," Syringa replied. "Goodnight, Lord Jupiter, and I am so happy, so very ... very happy to be here with ... you."

She raised her face as she spoke and it was a gesture of a child.

The Earl looked down at her and for a moment she thought there was a strange fire burning in his eyes. But it must have been an illusion in the light of a candle as he bent his head and kissed her on the forehead.

She would have reached out her arms to him, but he was walking across the room. He opened the door and went out.

For some mysterious reason that she could not explain, Syringa felt a sense of disappointment.

# Chapter Six

Syringa came running down the stairs.

As she did so she noted that the hand on the grand-father clock in the Hall had not yet reached half after eight.

She was early because she had woken almost with the dawn, to watch the sunshine peep between the curtains and feel excited at the thought of the day that lay ahead.

She would be with the Earl, they would ride together, they would talk! She found herself going over a whole list of subjects that she wished to discuss with him.

Although it was early it was already warm, and going downstairs Syringa carried her riding-jacket over her arm and her hat in her hand.

She wore her riding-skirt with several voluminous petti-coats and a blouse of white muslin inset with lace over which Nana had spent many laborious hours.

It had however been made two years before, and now it clung to her figure making it very obvious that she was no longer the child which at times she appeared to be.

As she reached the Hall she heard the sound of a horse moving away outside the front door, and then saw the Earl come walking up the steps, his top-hat on his head and a riding-whip in his gloved hand.

"Oh! You have already been riding!" she exclaimed, the disappointment obvious in her voice.

"I woke early," the Earl answered. "Our plans are changed. I wish to speak with you, Syringa."

Not waiting for her answer he walked ahead through the great marble Hall and entered his Study.

He crossed the room and stood with his back to the chimney-piece watching Syringa who had followed him. She paused just inside the door, a troubled expression in her grey eyes.

There was silence until Syringa said:

"Why have you changed our plans? I was so looking forward to riding with you this morning."

"I have decided to take you to London," the Earl replied.

"To London!"

There was sheer astonishment in the exclamation.

"I was thinking last night," the Earl continued, "that it was a mistake for me to have brought you to King's Keep. You will not mention to anyone that you have stayed here unchaperoned."

"But why? What does it matter? Who would be interested?" Syringa asked.

"Let me finish," the Earl said and his tone was severe. "You will go to London as my Ward. Our story is that you were left in my charge by your father on his death."

"I do not understand!" Syringa said. "Why are all these falsehoods necessary?"

"I have already sent a groom ahead," the Earl continued as if she had not spoken, "to ask my maternal grandmother, the Dowager Lady Hurlingham, to chaperone you. You will stay at Rothingham House and from there you will make your début into Society."

"No! No!" Syringa cried.

She moved across the room towards him.

"I have no desire to enter society," she declared. "I am ignorant of the social world and the people who inhabit it. Why should you wish me to go to London? Why should you take me away from here?"

"I have decided it is for your good," the Earl replied in a lofty tone. "You must have a chance, Syringa, to get to know the world in which you have been born and to meet men. After all, your acquaintance with the species until now has been somewhat limited."

"Why should I want to meet men?" Syringa asked.

The Earl did not answer and after a moment she asked in a low hesitating voice:

"Are you ... suggesting that I should ... marry? Is that a ... way of being ... rid of me?"

"I did not say that," the Earl answered sharply, "I merely pointed out that in your sheltered almost cloistered life, you have met very few people and certainly not any eligible bachelors."

Syringa stared at him, her eyes searching his face.

Then she walked across the room to the window to stand staring out blindly at the beauty of the lawns and the sunlit blossoms.

The Earl stood looking at her back, then sat down in a high-backed armchair still with his eyes on her. She turned round suddenly and ran towards him falling down on her knees beside his chair.

She threw back her head to look up at him.

"Please ... let us ... stay here," she pleaded, her voice intense and passionate. "We have been so ... happy, it has been so ... wonderful just to be with ... you! Do not ... spoil it! Let us remain at ... King's Keep."

The Earl looked down into her face for a moment and then he said, his voice surprisingly harsh:

"And do you really think such happiness would last? Would it not become boring for both of us?"

Syringa's eyes were stricken, it was almost as if he had hit her.

"You mean that ... you would be ... bored," she said in a whisper.

Very slowly she rose to her feet.

"I thought you seemed ... happy and I made you ... laugh. It has been so ... wonderful for ... me, but of course I ... understand you want other ... things."

"There are a diversity of entertainments in London," the Earl said.

"For you," Syringa replied, "but not for ... me. I will ... stay here."

The Earl's lips tightened.

"I have already explained, Syringa, that no-one is to know that you have been here even for two nights. You may be innocent but not so innocent as to think that a Lady should stay alone in a Gentleman's house unchaperoned."

There was silence until Syringa said in a very low voice:

"But you said I could not ... stay at the Manor. Where can I ... go?"

"You will obey me, Syringa," the Earl answered. "You will come to London, you will meet the *Beau Monde* under the chaperonage of my Grandmother, and you will enjoy yourself immensely. I have already given orders for the carriage to be brought round to the door in an hour's time. Go and change into a travelling dress."

Syringa turned to look at him, and she lifted her chin.

"I can give you, My Lord, a very good reason why I cannot ... come to London. I have no ... clothes!"

"That is something which will be easily remedied," the Earl answered, "You will be dressed as befits your position as my Ward."

"And ... you will ... pay for my ... gowns?" she asked in a shocked voice. "But of course not! How could I accept such a suggestion?"

For the first time she appeared to surprise the Earl.

"My Grandmother will meet the accounts, if that is what is troubling you," he said.

"But you will be paying!" Syringa said. "It is a gift I naturally cannot take from you."

The Earl still looked at her in continuing surprise, but she went on:

"Mama has told me that a Lady may accept flowers and bonbons as a present from a Gentleman. But never, never anything else, and certainly not an ... article of clothing!"

For the first time since he had entered the Library, there was a faint smile on the Earl's lips.

"Surely that is somewhat splitting hairs?" he asked. "You have already, Syringa, involved me in quite considerable expense. A few gowns can hardly matter one way or another."

"It is not just a question of money," Syringa replied with dignity, "I am sure you are wealthy enough not to notice a few guineas expended in fripperies. But I can not accept, in principle, even one gown from you."

"Your principles make life very difficult," the Earl complained. "First you attempt to starve yourself to death. Now apparently you wish me to take you to London and present you to the most critical society in the world, dressed – charmingly I admit – but in what will undoubtedly be considered a beggarly fashion."

"I should have thought, My Lord, that you are of such consequence that my clothes are of little import," Syringa retorted.

There was a flash of anger in her eyes which the Earl did not miss.

"Unfortunately," he replied and now he was drawling the words, "I have a rooted objection to being thought niggling or cheese-paring, especially towards someone who is my protégée and under my Guardianship."

"You mean people would criticise ... you?" Syringa asked. "But surely no-one would expect you to pay for the ... very clothes I wore?"

The Earl did not answer and after a moment she went on :

"I will not allow you to do such a thing ... whatever you may ... say! Mama would not approve and I know however ... persuasive you may ... sound, that it is ... wrong."

She gripped her fingers together as she spoke because it was hard to defy him, very hard not to accept what he asked.

The Earl looked at her for a moment then he turned and walked towards the door.

"Where are you going?" Syringa enquired.

"As I have already told you, Syringa, I am going to London," he replied. "I will make arrangements for you and your Nurse to return to the Manor. If we do not meet again, I thank you, Syringa, for the amusing hours I have spent in your company."

"If we do ... not meet ... again," Syringa repeated the words almost beneath her breath.

The Earl had put out his hand towards the door before he heard her footsteps running across the room behind him.

He waited and then a very small frightened little voice said:

"I will ... come to London with ... you, My Lord. I will ... accept ... your offer of some ... new ... gowns."

A week later Syringa, standing in Madame Bertin's Salon in Bond Street, thought that fitting gowns was more exhausting than spending a day in the saddle.

But the Dowager Lady Hurlingham, old though she might be, seemed impervious to fatigue when they were shopping.

Syringa felt at first that the Earl's grandmother was very awe-inspiring, but the Dowager had been a beauty in her youth, and if her looks had faded, her personality had become more perceptive.

She was autocratic but charming and extremely amusing, with a caustic wit which spared neither friend nor foe.

She had liked Syringa as soon as they met and was determined to make her a social success, not only because her grandson had demanded it of her.

"You are a good child," she said, "and that is more than I can say of most young wenches today!"

"What do they do which offends you?" Syringa enquired and received a voluble reply which made her laugh.

Her first days in London had been mostly spent in shops. She had never dreamt that a Lady of Fashion would require so many garments or such a varied collection of them.

But the Dowager Lady Hurlingham had been insistent that they must carry out the Earl's orders.

There were morning gowns and afternoon ones. There were magnificent and entrancing Robes de Soir to wear at Balls, Assemblies and Routs.

There were négligées in which to rest before dinner. There were riding-habits and mantles, shawls and wraps, and dozens of accessories which seemed to Syringa to grow and multiply day by day.

She could not help being thrilled at the difference such gowns had made to her appearance, and it seemed to her that not only the Dowager but everyone in the household was interested in seeing the country mouse transformed into a Town bird of paradise.

It was worth everything, even the discomfort of fittings, Syringa thought, to know that she had the Earl's approval.

The very first day when the Dowager had taken her shopping, she had driven back to Berkeley Square wearing a gown of pale jonquil yellow gauze which, fashioned by a master hand, seemed to transform her from an unobtrusive little figure into a ray of sunshine.

The large straw hat that accompanied it was tied under her chin with yellow satin ribbons and decorated with tiny yellow feathers encircling a low crown.

When she had looked at herself in the mirror at Madame Bertin's shop, Syringa had hardly recognised herself.

She had known then for the first time that women could use clothes like a weapon to enhance their loveliness and to get their own way!

As she stepped out of the carriage, she thought there was a gleam of admiration even in old Meadstone's eyes.

"Is His Lordship in?" she asked the butler as he took the Dowager's wrap.

"His Lordship's in the Library, Miss."

Without waiting Syringa ran across the Hall, and before a footman could open the door she entered the Library, her eyes alight with excitement.

The Earl was standing with his back to the chimney-piece and she flung wide her arms.

"My Lord, behold a miracle!" she cried. "Do you know me? For if I met myself in the street, I swear I should not recognise myself."

It was only as her voice rang out gay and excited that she realised that the Earl was not alone.

"You look entrancing," he said.

Turning to his Grandmother who had just entered the room behind Syringa he added:

"My congratulations, Grandmama, I always knew your taste was infallible."

"You did not set me a very difficult task," the Dowager replied. "Syringa looks attractive in everything."

Syringa glanced round gratefully, but she was conscious all the time of the woman sitting on the sofa beside the hearth. She was a vision of beauty, more elegant and more attractive than anyone she had ever seen in her life before.

"Is this your little ward, Ancelin?" the Vision enquired.

Syringa was aware that behind the gentleness of the tone there was a touch of acid.

"Yes, indeed," the Earl replied, "let me introduce you. Miss Syringa Melton – Lady Elaine Wilmot, and I think, Elaine, you know my Grandmother."

Lady Elaine rose gracefully to her feet.

"Yes, of course," she said, "we met last year M'am when you were staying here with Ancelin, but not encumbered with so much responsibility as now."

"A responsibility I much enjoy," the Dowager replied, as if she had been challenged.

"Well I for one am thankful that I am too old to be wearied by the cheeping of unfledged chits at débutante balls," Lady Elaine declared. "And so is Ancelin, unless he intends to sit amongst the Dowagers."

"I might even do that," the Earl said with a smile.

"And leave me alone?" Lady Elaine asked plaintively. "You could not be so unkind! Besides how should I fare without you?"

She looked up at him provocatively, her dark eyes glinting, her red lips pouting. Syringa suddenly felt gauche and very unsophisticated.

She was aware of the exotic perfume which Lady Elaine used. She realised that every gesture of her white hands weighed down with rings, every movement of her sinuous body, was a deliberate calculated allure.

And she? She could only be herself – a green girl from the country.

She looked towards the Dowager for guidance, and as if the older woman understood her plea she said:

"We must not interrupt you, Ancelin. Syringa and I have many things to do. We have only just begun our shopping."

"How amusing it must be for you," Lady Elaine said. "I have always longed to be able to shop knowing that the price was of no consequence and there was a long purse to meet my every need."

There was no mistaking the sting behind the words and the Dowager replied:

"I am sure you have little cause to complain. I noticed at Madame Bertin's quite a number of boxes awaiting delivery which bore your name."

Lady Elaine flashed her a glance of sheer hatred and then said too quickly to sound plausible:

"A few gowns I was having altered! And one which was most regrettably torn the other night at Carlton House."

"Of course," the Dowager replied, "we all have to practise these little economies. Come, Syringa!"

Syringa hurried to open the door. As the older woman swept out she looked back at the Earl. She had hoped that he might be looking up at her, but Lady Elaine's hand was on his arm ad her face was upturned to his.

"I was going to ask you, Ancelin," she heard Lady Elaine say, "to be very generous and give..."

Syringa waited for no more. She hurried out of the Library and followed the Dowager upstairs.

As they reached the first floor and were out of hearing of the footmen in the Hall, the Earl's Grandmother said:

"A most forward young woman! I always disliked her father."

"She is very ... beautiful," Syringa said, and wondered why her voice sounded so miserable.

"Beauty can often be a snare and an illusion," the Dowager retorted, "as many a good man has found to his cost."

Syringa longed to ask if the Earl too would discover that, but she knew she could not bring herself to say the words.

Besides was it not obvious that he found Lady Elaine very attractive?

She found herself wondering over and over again what Lady Elaine was asking the Earl to give her. She knew she would never be brave enough to ask him what it might be.

In the afternoons she was taken by the Dowager to Receptions and to call on Ladies of Quality.

In the evenings there were dinner parties at Rothingham House, and usually the Earl accompanied them afterwards to the great houses of London – Devonshire, Lansdown, Chesterfield, Londonderry, Dudley.

Syringa found herself often over-awed but at the same time interested and delighted by the grandeur, the tradition and the pageantry of these mansions.

The flunkeys with their plush trousers, white silk stockings and powdered hair; the Major-Domos resplendent in their gold lace, the tables and sideboards groaning with gold and silver; the huge Dining Rooms and the silk panelled Salons all provided a dramatic background for their owners.

Never had she imagined that women could be so beautiful or men so witty and elegant.

She was quiet and unassuming in her manner as befitted a young girl, but both the Earl and his grandmother noticed that she could talk charmingly and without being tiresomely shy to anyone who wished to converse with her.

It also seemed that people naturally gravitated towards Syringa.

It was as if she drew them to her side, and they would discuss serious subjects rather than the frivolous frothy gossip with which the rest of the party passed the time.

"What were you talking about to the Prime Minister?" the Earl asked.

They were driving back from a reception at Stafford House.

"Mr. William Pitt was explaining to me the difficulties of the Local Elections," Syringa answered, "and telling me what he is advocating for Electoral Reform."

"Are you interested in such things?" the Earl asked in amazement.

"I think any subject is interesting if the person is knowledgeable and vitally concerned with it," Syringa replied. "Mr. Pitt was extremely interesting and he has promised that next week, if your Grandmother will permit it, he will arrange for me to visit the House of Commons so that I can watch the proceedings from the Ladies Gallery."

"I will take you to the Lords if that would interest you," the Earl offered.

"Oh, will you really?" Syringa cried, "I would love that!"

"You are in London to enjoy yourself," the Earl answered, "and I should have thought dancing was more to your liking."

"I enjoy that too," Syringa said, "but you never ask me to dance."

"I do not dance," the Earl answered firmly. "Like Grandmama, I prefer a game of cards while you and the young are enjoying themselves."

"Perhaps I could learn to play with you," Syringa suggested.

"No, you are too young," the Earl replied. "Keep to the dance-floor, Syringa, which is where you should be."

At the next Ball to which he accompanied Syringa, he noticed that while at first she danced obediently with the gentlemen who asked her, she later disappeared into the garden with the young Marquis of Thanet.

His first impulse was to warn her that such conduct might give rise to unfavourable comment.

Then he restrained himself from interfering and the effort made him exceedingly disagreeable.

It was two days later that the Earl heard the Library door open and a voice say:

"Are you alone? Could I speak with Your Lordship for a moment?"

He glanced round and saw Syringa dressed in a pale green gown.

It made him think of the shrubs coming into bloom at King's Keep as they were the first time he met her.

He noticed, as she crossed the big Library towards him, that her silken skirts rustled like the trees in Monk's Wood.

"You wish to see me," the Earl said abruptly. "Well, as it happens I was just going to send for you. The Marquis of Thanet has asked me, Syringa, if he may pay his addresses to you."

"I told him not to!" Syringa exclaimed. "How can he be so tiresome and waste your time!"

"Waste my time!" the Earl ejaculated in surprise.

"I have already told the Marquis that I will not marry him."

The Earl rose to his feet and walked across the room, almost as if he was giving himself time in which to think.

When he reached the hearth-rug he stood still and asked:

"Am I understanding you correctly? The Marquis of Thanet has asked you for your hand in marriage?"

"He has asked me several times," Syringa answered, "and on each occasion I have given him the same answer. He has only come to you because he hopes you will further his suit."

"Come and sit down, Syringa," the Earl said and seated himself in an arm-chair.

He crossed his legs and sat back. His eyes, very blue in

his sun-tanned face, seemed to Syringa to be looking deep into her heart as if he would find the truth.

"Why have you refused the Marquis?" he asked.

"It is quite simple," she replied with a smile, "I do not love him!"

"Have you told my Grandmother that he has proposed to you?" the Earl asked.

"I did not exactly tell her," Syringa answered, "but she guessed it from something the Marquis said, and she told me I was to accept him. She was very insistent that it was the best offer I was ever likely to receive."

"Grandmama is right!" the Earl said. "Thanet is a Marquis and immensely wealthy. He is also a sportsman and a man liked by other men. This is important, Syringa.'

"I too like His Lordship," Syringa answered, "and I have told him so, only I do not wish to marry him."

"But he is a Marquis," the Earl repeated, "I thought all young women wished above all else for an important title."

A dimple appeared at the corner of Syringa's mouth.

"Why?" she asked. "Like diamonds you cannot eat them!"

The Earl laughed before he said:

"As your Guardian I should do as Thanet expects of me: make you accept such an advantageous proposal."

"And as my friend . . ." Syringa said in a low voice, "you know quite well that I will marry . . . no-one whom I do not . . . love."

There was silence.

"And have you found no-one to love since you have been in London?"

Syringa shook her head.

The Earl looked at her as if he could hardly believe she spoke the truth. Then he said:

"Very well, Syringa, if that is your wish, I will inform the Marquis that the choice is entirely yours."

"Thank you," Syringa said. "And now may I tell you what I came to say?"

"Of course," the Earl replied. "I must apologise, Syringa, for not allowing you to speak first. It is a lady's privilege."

"I wanted to wish you many ... happy returns of the ... day, My Lord," Syringa said in a shy voice, "and I have brought you ... a present."

"A present?" the Earl exclaimed.

"Your Grandmama told me two or three days ago that your birthday was today," she explained, "and I have made something for you."

She rose as she spoke and handed him a parcel done up with a bow of red ribbon.

As if the excitement of waiting for him to open it was too intense for her to stand aloof, she knelt down at his side her eyes shining.

"It is many years since I have had a birthday present," the Earl said slowly. "In fact I am getting so old that I keep my birthday a secret."

"You are thirty-two!" Syringa smiled, "but you need not have so many candles on your cake."

She put her fingers to her mouth.

"Oh, it was to be a secret!"

The Earl undid the bow of ribbon. The parcel was very thin and square. He opened it and found a picture of a brown and white spaniel.

There was silence as he looked at it. Then as if she could not bear the suspense Syringa added:

"Is it ... is it at all like ... Judith?"

"It is very like her," the Earl answered.

He realised Syringa had used as a model one of the prints which hung on the walls in the passages. The picture was painted in water-colours and he knew she must have spent a great deal of time on its execution.

"Did you really do this all yourself?" he asked.

"I used to sketch to please Mama," Syringa answered. "But I am afraid I shall never be a real artist: I am always in too much of a hurry. But it does ... please you?"

She looked up at him anxiously.

"It pleases me very much," the Earl said. "Thank you, Syringa, I shall treasure it always."

She gave a little sigh of relief.

"I am so glad! I wanted to give you something ... that was all mine. It would not have been the same if I had paid for it with ... your money."

"This is indeed all yours," he said. "Thank you again, Syringa."

His eyes met hers and for a moment it seemed to her as if something strange passed between them, something she did not understand but which made her quiver.

Then, as she felt rather shy and at the same time strangely excited, the Earl rose to his feet.

"I have a present for you, Syringa," he said.

He walked to his desk, opened a drawer and drew out a velvet-covered box.

"Tomorrow we dine at Carlton House," he said, "and I think you will find this will embellish the beautiful gown which Grandmama tells me she has had chosen for you."

He put the box into Syringa's hands. She opened it and then gave an exclamation.

Lying on the black velvet was a spray of flowers. Fashioned with diamonds they glittered and shimmered and the blossoms even moved at the touch of Syringa's fingers.

She stood looking down at it, and then as she did not speak the Earl looking at her bent head asked:

"You do not like it?"

"It is beautiful ... very beautiful," she said slowly.

"Then what is wrong?" he enquired.

"I do not ... wish to ... hurt you."

"To hurt me?"

She looked up at him, her eyes troubled.

"You must ... understand," she said, "you must ... realise that I cannot ... accept this gift."

"They are diamonds, Syringa. All women like diamonds."

"They may like them," Syringa answered, "but they

should not accept them from ... a man to whom they are not ... married."

For a moment the Earl was still. Then he said:

"Are we once again concerned with your principles? As you well know, Syringa, I find them extremely irritating."

Syringa put the diamond brooch down on the desk.

"It is not ... only ... that," she whispered.

"Then what is it?" the Earl asked.

"I would rather ... not tell ... you."

"I am afraid I must insist on a reasonable explanation," he said. "You made an absurd fuss about accepting your gowns from me. But we overcame that difficulty, and I am sure you have found that I was right in saying that you must be suitably dressed to appear upon the social scene."

He waited as if he expected an answer.

"Yes ... you were ... right," Syringa agreed, "and I am very ... grateful for all the lovely clothes you have ... given me. I have thanked you for them and I shall go on thanking you! But a diamond brooch is ... different."

"How? In what way?" the Earl asked.

She heard the irritation in his tone and Syringa twisted her fingers together miserably.

How could she explain to him, she wondered, what Lady Elaine had said to her only a few days after her arrival in London.

She had been alone in the Drawing-Room waiting for the Dowager, when Lady Elaine had been announced. She had appeared more glamorous, more beautiful than ever.

Her gown was elaborate as befitted her status of a married woman, her hair was a mass of intricate curls, and the hat that she wore on her head was a riot of flame-coloured feathers.

"Alone?" Lady Elaine had asked in surprise. "Where is the delectable Earl?"

"I do not think His Lordship is expected until later," Syringa answered.

"It is of no consequence," Lady Elaine said, "because I wish to speak to you."

"To me?" Syringa enquired in surprise.

"Yes you," Lady Elaine answered. "Naturally I am interested in anyone who is staying in Ancelin's house. We are so close, we do so many things together that it surprised me that he did not ask my opinion about you before you arrived."

"Things were . . . arranged in rather a . . . hurry," Syringa said uncomfortably.

"I know that," Lady Elaine agreed. "And I have told Ancelin that I forgive him. After all, although you are a very pretty child, I can afford to be generous. Ancelin may offer you his hospitality – but he gives me so much – so very much more."

Lady Elaine had spoken softly but there appeared to be a deliberate under-current in her words.

"What do you mean?" Syringa asked bluntly.

"I mean, dear, and it is wise for you to know this from the very beginning in case you should have any illusions about His Lordship, that he loves me. He has loved me for a very long time."

Syringa drew in her breath and then as she did not speak Lady Elaine continued:

"But of course you must have been aware of it! Everyone in London knows it. Our names are always coupled together!"

She saw the expression on Syringa's face and rose to her feet – a satisfied smile on her lips.

"I will not trouble to wait for the Dowager," she said, "and anyway I shall see her at the Ball tonight. We are all dining in the same party."

She paused a moment. Then she added:

"I am so looking forward to Ancelin seeing my new gown because it matches the ruby necklace he gave me. Such a lovely present, one of the many in which he expresses his love for me."

She went from the room and Syringa wondered why, when she was gone, she felt as though someone had turned a knife in her heart.

Now, instead of the diamonds glittering in their velvet box she could only see the necklace of blood-red rubies, fiery and somehow evil against the whiteness of Lady Elaine's neck.

"I am waiting, Syringa," the Earl said.

His voice made her start because her thoughts had been far away.

"Waiting," she repeated.

"For an explanation," he said, "and I would like the truth."

There was a pause before Syringa said in a low hesitating voice.

"You give ... jewels to ... other women. Perhaps ... they are ... able to give you ... something ... in return. But I can give you ... nothing and ... therefore I would not be under a further ... obligation to ... you, My Lord."

Her head was bent and she did not see the expression in the Earl's eyes.

"You mean," he said quietly after a moment, "you do not like taking without giving."

"No ... no."

"And you are perhaps aware that I have given jewels to Lady Elaine."

"She ... told ... me ... so."

There was a pause before Syringa continued.

"Lady Elaine must do as ... she thinks ... right, but I would ... rather not accept ... the brooch ... beautiful though ... it is."

There was a little throb in her voice as if tears were not far away.

It was hard to fight the Earl and she knew that if he wished he could force her into accepting the present, to browbeat her as he had done before into obeying him.

The Earl put out his hand and shut the lid of the velvet box with a decisive click.

"Very well, Syringa," he said, "I will not plague you. Instead I will offer you something else. It might please you."

She looked up at him wide-eyed. Her face was very pale in case he was incensed with her.

The Earl sat down at his desk and taking a key opened a bottom drawer. From it he drew out a square jewel-box and set it in front of him.

"I have here," he said, "the jewels that belonged personally to my mother. They are of little value or my father would undoubtedly have sold them. When she died she left them to me for – my wife."

He inserted the key in the lock and lifted the lid.

"I would not give them away," he went on, "but I would like you, Syringa to borrow a brooch and wear it for as long as it pleases you."

The light came back into Syringa's eyes.

"Could I do that?" she asked. "I would be very honoured and very proud to wear anything that belonged to your mother. I will take good care of it and whenever you want you will have it back."

She leant over the Earl's shoulder, looking into the jewel-box. There were several brooches, but there was one particularly that took her fancy.

It was of three little flowers fashioned of turquoise. In the centre of each there was a diamond and the stalks and a small leaf were also made of brilliants.

She touched it gently with her finger and the Earl drew it from the box.

"I thought this was the one you would like."

"It reminds me of our Secret Place," Syringa said, "of the blue periwinkles that one can find in the grass, and there are also blue forget-me-nots."

"Then this undoubtedly is the brooch you must wear," the Earl said. "I am sure it will bring you luck."

138

"I am so lucky already," Syringa smiled, "I cannot believe that I could be more fortunate."

"Are you quite sure about that?" the Earl enquired.

"Quite sure!" she answered. "But perhaps this brooch will make something wonderful happen to me."

She pushed the pin through the front of her dress as she spoke.

"Is that straight?" she asked.

"Not quite," he answered.

He took the brooch from her and pinned it where the low decolletage of her gown just hid the little valley between her breasts.

She felt his fingers touch her skin and a quiver ran through her like quick silver.

It was strange, she thought, and she could not quite understand or explain the sensation.

The brooch was fastened.

"I like to think of you wearing something which belonged to my mother," the Earl said.

"How can I thank you?" Syringa asked. "It is your birthday, and yet you have given me a present."

She touched the brooch with her fingers.

Then impulsively she bent forward and pressed her lips against the Earl's cheek.

"Thank you ... thank you, Lord Jupiter," she whispered, "not only for the brooch but for ... everything else."

Then before he could answer, before he could rise to his feet, as if overcome with shyness she ran from the room.

Syringa went upstairs conscious that she could still feel the firm warmth of the Earl's cheek against her lips. She remembered how the first time they met he had kissed her, and now she had kissed him!

Somehow it was different, although she was not quite certain how.

She opened the door of the Drawing-Room expecting to find the Dowager there and wishing to display her new brooch.

But to her consternation she saw sitting together on the sofa, their heads very close, Lady Elaine and Ninian Roth.

She had met the Earl's cousin already on several occasions, and for some reason she could not explain to herself had disliked him on sight.

A man nearing forty he was, Syringa had learnt, heir-presumptive to the title. There was something suave and slightly slimy about him.

Very thin with a long pointed nose, he had eyes which seemed always to hold secrets that he dare not reveal.

Ninian Roth was dressed in the height of fashion and was a Dandy who wore an elaborate amount of jewellery.

He was obviously *persona grata* with all the fashionable hostesses, and Syringa had heard a number of people speaking warmly of his charm and his accomplishments.

"It is foolish of me," she thought, now seeing him across the room, "but I do not trust him! Why is he talking so intimately to Lady Elaine?"

She had then a quite unaccountable feeling that the Earl might be in danger. Then Lady Elaine saw her in the doorway and held out her hand.

"Syringa!" she exclaimed, "how delightful to see you! We were just talking about you."

"Talking about me?" Syringa enquired.

"Yes, indeed! Ninian was saying what a success you have been since you came to London, and how many people have congratulated him on a new and charming member of the family."

"Yes, that is true," Ninian Roth interposed. "I really feel as if we have adopted you. And as you are an orphan why should we not do so?"

"I am quite content as I am," Syringa replied, hoping it did not sound rude.

"But of course you are!" Lady Elaine agreed. "We are only joking! But Ninian predicts a very exciting future for you, Syringa. I wonder whom you will marry?"

"I have no wish to marry anyone," Syringa said quietly.

"You must not tell that to the Dowager!" Lady Elaine exclaimed in mock dismay. "She is making such plans for you and already I am quite certain she has in mind many eligible and important *partis*."

"I think I will go and find Her Ladyship," Syringa said a little breathlessly.

"No, no wait a moment!" Lady Elaine said. "We were just going to tell you something so amusing, were we not, Ninian?"

"Yes, indeed," Ninian Roth replied. "I am sure you would find it great fun."

"What is it?" Syringa asked.

"Ninian has found a new fortune-teller," Lady Elaine explained. "And she is not only a fortune-teller, but extremely clever at telling character."

"I do not want to have my fortune told," Syringa replied, "I do not want to know the future ... I am quite content with the ... present."

"Oh you cannot spoil our fun!" Lady Elaine protested. "We have all consulted Madame Zelobia. All you have to do, Syringa, is to write something on a piece of paper. She can tell from your handwriting not only your future, but your past, and all the characteristics that make you what you are."

"It is a very old science as a matter of fact," Ninian said.

"I would much rather ... not do it," Syringa said.

"How could you be so unkind to Ninian when he has gone to so much trouble and persuaded her to do you," Lady Elaine enquired.

"To do me! Why me?" Syringa asked.

"Because we want to test Madame. You see she knows too much about me, too much about Ninian, too much about Ancelin! We are talked about, we are written about in the newspapers. People know all our secrets."

She made a wide gesture with her white hands.

"But you are new, and if she is right where you are concerned, well we shall know she is not a fraud. Can you not see that?"

"Yes I ... understand," Syringa said slowly.

"Mrs. Fitzherbert has promised that she will go to her, and that means the Prince of Wales will go too. So you see, Syringa, we have to be very careful not to recommend anyone who is not absolutely honest and above-board."

"Of course not," Syringa agreed.

"Then do what Ninian asks," Lady Elaine said.

Ninian Roth produced a plain piece of paper.

"All you have to do," he explained, "is to write your name. It is not very difficult is it?"

"Not really."

She did not know why, but she felt curiously reluctant to do what they asked.

"It is stupid of me," she thought, "but I do not want to be mixed up with fortune-tellers where Lady Elaine and Ninian Roth are concerned."

She felt there was some ulterior reason why they wanted her to be involved. They had never seemed anxious for her company or been interested in her before – so why now? But it was impossible to extricate herself without being positively rude.

"Just sign your name here," Ninian Roth said pointing to the centre of the white parchment.

He walked as he spoke to the *secretaire* which stood in the corner of the Drawing-Room. Sitting down in the writing chair, Syringa picked up a white quill pen.

She hesitated. Ninian Roth was waiting and she had the absurd feeling that he was willing her to do what he wished.

Slowly, in her small exquisite writing, Syringa wrote her name.

"And now I have a splendid idea!" Ninian Roth exclaimed. "Write another name and the fortune-teller will think it is another person. We will not tell her it is you, and if she describes two entirely different characters, then we shall know she is a fraud!"

"But of course!" Lady Elaine cried. "How brilliant of you, Ninian!"

Syringa sat with the quill pen in her hand staring from one to the other.

"Go on," Ninian Roth prompted, "write a name – any name at the bottom of the page."

"I cannot think of one!" Syringa said stupidly.

"Then let me think for you," he said. "What about Elizabeth Witheringham? It sounds very different to Syringa Melton does it not?"

Slowly Syringa wrote "Elizabeth Witheringham" at the place he indicated.

"Now this will be a real test," Lady Elaine said. "They say the Prince is very credulous and I would not like him to be misled by a charlatan. Some of these seers into the future are, I am told, completely unscrupulous."

"That is why I would rather not go to them," Syringa said rising from the *secretaire*.

"We will never bother you to go to another one," Ninian Roth said.

There was something in the way he said it which made Syringa quite inexplicably feel afraid.

"I would much rather not go to this one," she said quickly. "Please let me tear up the paper."

"I am sure that would be very unlucky," he replied. "You are committed now to help us, you cannot draw back."

"But why? It is not really too late is it?" Syringa said.

"Oh really you are being too nonsensical!" Lady Elaine exclaimed. "You are frightening the child, Ninian. It is after all only a game – fun for us all. Do not be a spoil-sport, Syringa, I am sure Ancelin will think it most amusing."

There was nothing else Syringa could say, and yet as she went upstairs to her own bedroom, she was worried.

She did not know why, but she had a distinct presentiment of evil.

# Chapter Seven

The Prince of Wales was getting foxed. The Earl thought that it was not surprising considering that the Duke of Norfolk was his host.

Had the Earl known that after dinner at Carlton House the evening's entertainment was to be provided by the Duke of Norfolk, he would not have accepted the Prince's most pressing invitation to be present.

The Duke of Norfolk was sixteen years older than the Prince and had been a celebrated drunkard since he was a boy.

A very ill educated man, he had however a native intelligence and a biting wit which made him heartily disliked by a large number of his contemporaries. To the Prince he was however an intimate friend.

The dinner at Carlton House had been a replica of innumerable dinners the Earl had attended in the last three years.

No ladies were invited and the guests consisted of the Prince's more riotous and ill-famed friends whose company caused him to be parodied continually in Gillray's caricatures.

The fourth Marquess of Queensberry was a very much older man, yet the Prince seemed to enjoy his company.

Immensely rich and selfish, he was short of stature, sharp-looking, very irritable and swore like ten thousand troopers.

He was also a dedicated whore-monger, and it was said there was not a Lady of Quality in the whole of London who had not at some time been the object of his advances.

The Marquess received a lot of rebuffs, it was true, although, as he said himself, he also enjoyed a great many successes.

He was at the same time one of the most polished gentlemen of his day: he had a passion for music and a taste for literature and the fine arts. There was in fact some justification for the Prince's partiality for him.

In the company of these noblemen it was natural to find the wild Barrymore brothers, and all three of them were seated round the big table in the Dining-Room of Carlton House with its silver walls supported by columns of red and yellow granite.

The seventh Earl of Barrymore was doing his best to dissipate a fortune worth over twenty thousand a year. He was so depraved and so dissolute that he was known to all and sundry as "Hellgate".

The stories of the escapades of his friends were whispered in every London Drawing-Room and embellished in every tavern, while the newspapers found him an inexhaustible source of scandal with which to fill their columns.

The Earl's elder brother, the Honourable and Reverend Augustus Barry, was a compulsive gambler, ever on the edge of being sent to prison, and was inevitably known as "Newgate". The younger brother, who had a club foot, was dubbed "Cripplegate".

The three brothers had a strange sense of humour.

One of their jokes was to race down to Brighton in their coach, stopping to uproot or displace sign-posts or to scream "Murder! Rape! Unhand me, villain!" to all who would listen.

When their coach was overtaken and stopped by travellers who believed a murder was really being committed, they would jump out to insult and physically assault the good Samaritans.

When they stayed in Brighton, the three brothers called themselves 'The Merry Mourners', and carrying a coffin at night used to knock on the doors of respectable citizens and tradesmen and tell the terrified maid-servant who opened the door that they had come to remove the corpse.

'Cripplegate' on one occasion rode his horse up the staircase of Mrs. Fitzherbert's house right into the attic, where he left it to be brought down by two blacksmiths.

On another occasion 'Hellgate' dressed up in the clothes of his cook and sang a serenade at three o'clock in the morning underneath Mrs. Fitzherbert's bed-room window.

It was strange that after such behaviour the Prince should still go on calling the brothers his friends, but they amused him although the Earl of Rothingham found them oafish and at times repugnant.

Another guest at the Prince's table was Sir John Lade, a disreputable man who however had an amusing wit. He had inherited a huge fortune from brewing and he advised the Prince on the management of his racing stables.

He was married to an attractive but loud-mouthed courtesan named Letitia who had numbered the Duke of York among her lovers.

Besides these notorious characters there was at the party a collection of the Prince's hangers-on and toadies, who flattered him to his face and sniggered at him behind his back.

"It is a pity," the Earl said to himself, "that the Prince's unerring taste where works of art are concerned is not extended to his choice of friends."

He had only to look at the walls of Carlton House to confirm the truth of this observation.

The Prince's flair for the Dutch Masters he had collected, his patronage of modern artists like Lawrence, Reynolds and Gainsborough would, the Earl was convinced, be acclaimed by posterity.

But his Royal Highness's companions would go down to history as parasites, drunken reprobates and licentious libertines.

"I wish I had not come!" the Earl thought to himself at Carlton House as the drink flowed too freely and there would inevitably be too many over-rich courses.

And he said it to himself again when the Prince insisted that they must all proceed to the party that the Duke of Norfolk was giving at The White House.

This was the most famous and the most exclusive brothel-cum-gambling house in the whole of London. Its shrewd proprietor was clever in providing everything that a Gentleman of Fashion needed for a relaxed and pleasurable evening. The place itself was attractive, well decorated and well managed.

The private rooms had a charm of their own. There were murals of half-naked nymphs pursued by satyrs, and each room had a special motif to make them distinguishable.

There was the Silver Room, the Gold Room, Persephone's Bower and innumerable others, each served by powdered and gold laced flunkeys and provided with most alluring women if also the most expensive.

The Silver Room where the Duke was giving his party, was octagonal in shape. There were gaming-tables for the Prince and a number of soft cushioned couches arranged in alcoves for those who had other ideas of enjoyment.

The wine was of the best and by the time the Prince and his friends arrived somewhat unsteadily from Carlton House the theatres were over, and a number of the Corps de Ballet were at the Duke's invitation already waiting.

The Earl was relieved to see that Michelle was not amongst them.

However, there was, he noted, the little red-head whose acquaintance he had planned to make when he returned from the country.

He remembered vaguely telling someone that he was interested in her, and he was surprised to realise that the Duke had taken more trouble than usual to pander to the taste of his guests and of himself in particular.

He might have thought such an idea was too far-fetched, had not the Duke immediately on their arrival brought the pretty red-head up to him and said:

"Here is someone who is very anxious to meet you, Rothingham. May I present Lottie Strasner, who, as I am sure you can guess, comes from Vienna."

Lottie, without making any pretence of formality, slipped her arm into the Earl's and drew him aside to sit with her on one of the couches.

"I have wanted – oh so much – to meet you for a long time, M'Lord," she said.

She had a rather attractive voice with just a trace of a broken accent.

"May I ask why?" the Earl enquired good-humouredly.

She fluttered her eyelashes as she replied:

"I am told you are generous, My Lord, very generous to those whom you like."

It was an answer that the Earl might have expected, and yet it jarred on him.

Only that afternoon Lady Elaine had attempted to persuade him to give her a ruby bracelet which matched the necklace on which he had expended quite a considerable amount of money.

"I would not press you if I were not so afraid that it will be sold to someone else," she pleaded. "It is in the window of a shop in Bond Street, and I am sure you would wish to give me something which would delight me more than anything else!"

The Earl was extremely generous when it pleased him, but like most other men, he disliked being forced into a generosity that did not come naturally.

He had not made love to Lady Elaine since he had returned to London, and he could not help feeling that she was being exceedingly greedy.

He knew that waiting on his secretary's desk for his approval were an abnormal number of bills for gowns, hats and other articles of clothing.

"I will think about it," he said.

"How kind you are, how sweet!" Lady Elaine had said, putting her arm round his neck to draw his head down to hers.

When almost unwillingly his lips were near, she said softly:

"You have been neglecting me, Ancelin. I have been waiting for you – waiting every night this week."

"I have been busy," the Earl said evasively.

"With your little protégée?" she asked, and somehow it was like the hiss of a snake.

The Earl had removed her arms.

"I hope you will be kind to Syringa," he said sharply. "She knows no-one in London and I wish her to enjoy herself."

"But of course," Lady Elaine replied, "and we must enjoy ourselves too. I miss you, Ancelin."

The Earl looked at his watch.

"I have an appointment at White's," he said coldly, "so I am afraid you must excuse me."

"And you will think about the bracelet?" Lady Elaine asked softly.

"I will think about it," he replied.

Now sitting on the sofa at the White House with Lottie Strasner's face upturned to his, the Earl wondered if all women were so avaricious. Were gowns and jewels all they really wanted from a man?

Then he heard a little voice saying hesitatingly:

"Perhaps ... they are ... able to give you ... something ... in return. But I can give you ... nothing ..."

Syringa was different from the others and he thought too that because she was so fragile and gentle, she made every other woman seem coarse and hard.

She was like a drawing and only the soft lines of a master hand could do justice to the spirituality of her face and her large eyes.

Only a pencil could portray the strange magic of her shadowy hair or the sensitive curve of her lips.

Lottie, with her red hair, mascara'ed eyelids and crimson mouth, looked somehow grotesque in comparison, while Lady Elaine's beauty, outstanding though it was, had no subtlety about it.

The Earl glanced towards the gaming-tables.

Charles James Fox, the brilliant politician and compulsive gambler, had joined the Prince. It was surprising that the young Prince admired him so much.

Paunchy, untidy, graceless, with a swarthy skin, a double chin and black shaggy eyebrows, Mr. Fox was a hard drinker who had taken over two of the Prince's former mistresses.

But he was also a man of amazing charm and brilliant intellect. His conversation was entertaining and his friendship for the Heir to the Throne, thirteen years younger than himself, was not merely useful politically, it was sincere.

But with Fox at the party the Earl knew that the gaming would go on until dawn.

It was a mistake for the Prince to gamble. He was already heavily in debt and he seldom won at cards.

The Earl knew however there was nothing he could do to prevent the Prince staying up all night with his friend Charles Fox, both of them throwing money they neither of them could afford on to the green baize tables.

A band was playing romantically in a minstrel's gallery screened with rose covered trellis work, so that they could not be seen.

Those of the Duke's guests who could still stand on their feet were dancing with the ladies who appeared to be shedding quite a number of their diaphanous garments as they twirled around the room.

Others on the couches, were behaving with a voluptuous indiscretion which was growing more abandoned every moment.

Two pretty members of the Corps de Ballet astride a couple of gentlemen were racing them across the floor to the accompaniment of a horsey commentary from those who had placed a wager on the event.

It was an exhibition which the Earl knew would be repeated again later in the evening, when the participants would wear far less clothing.

Whips would then be carried by the riders and spurs attached to their busy little heels.

Flunkeys with trays of crystal glasses filled to the brim with champagne or burgundy, kept passing amongst the guests so there was never a moment that their thirst might not be assuaged.

"You like me – yes?" the Earl heard Lottie say, and realised she was still clinging closely to his arm, her red head resting against his shoulder.

He brought his eyes back to her and noticed she used a perfume that was popular amongst the members of her profession, but was one for which he had a strong dislike.

It was over-pungent and it reminded him all too forcibly of several unfortunate episodes in the East which he hoped to forget.

He straightened himself on the sofa moving away from Lottie, feeling her proximity was too close and too familiar. He decided he was definitely not interested in her.

"You do not answer," she said provocatively. "Why do you not kiss me, M'Lord, and then – I show you how happy we can be – together."

"My apologies," the Earl said slowly, "but I have to leave."

"You have to – leave?"

The question was incredulous.

"I wish to do so!" the Earl replied.

He rose to his feet as he spoke, and moving slowly and without a hurry through the dancers walked towards the door.

As he reached it there was a sudden shrill scream of excitement from a dishevelled little dancer who was being pursued by two Bucks. She was heading straight towards the Earl and he stepped adroitly on one side to avoid her. She ran past him still screaming, the Bucks in hot pursuit.

The Earl glanced towards the gaming table: the Prince absorbed in his cards had not even raised his head at the noise, nor had Charles Fox.

The Earl opened the door and let himself out.

His coach was waiting and he drove back to Berkeley Square, asking himself as he went why the evening had proved so boring and why such antics no longer amused him.

He had to admit that he had been progressively disenchanted for some time with the excesses and orgies that the Prince of Wales's friends found so entertaining.

The Earl had never been promiscuous in his love-making. When he had a mistress he kept her discreetly in a house where he visited her when it suited him.

The idea of a rough and tumble in public such as he had just seen at the White House disgusted him.

As far as he was concerned, he would not so lower himself.

A mistress from the Corps de Ballet was one thing, but Lady Elaine was another, and driving him the Earl admitted to himself that, as far as he was concerned, the affaire was over.

She had excited him, he had desired her, and he had certainly paid heavily for such delights as she could give him.

But he had no wish to continue with a liaison which no longer gave him any pleasure and which he was beginning to find irksome.

Lady Elaine presumed too much. She was in and out of Rothingham House as if she already owned it.

She was possessive in public, she was deliberately indiscreet about their relationship, wishing everyone to know of their love affair so that eventually, the Earl thought grimly, he would be forced by public opinion into declaring himself.

"She will be disappointed," he vowed. "I have no intention of marrying her!"

The only difficulty was how he was to make it clear to Lady Elaine that she no longer had any claim upon him.

He stepped out at Rothingham House to find lights blazing, a number of the carriages outside and half a dozen footmen in attendance in the Hall.

He then remembered that his Grandmother had said she was entertaining that night.

It probably was a dinner-party, the Earl thought, with some young people for Syringa and a few of the Dowager's special cronies to play cards afterwards.

It was an hour after midnight, but there was still a large number of hats and cloaks in the Hall. The Earl handed his own hat to Meadstone and walked upstairs to the Salon.

There were two card-tables still occupied by the more elderly guests.

There were several younger people sitting talking on sofas, and Lady Elaine and Ninian Roth were playing piquet at a table near the door.

Lady Elaine saw the Earl first and threw out her arm in a welcoming gesture.

"Ancelin, how delightful!" she exclaimed. "When I heard you were dining at Carlton House, I despaired of seeing you this evening."

"I left early," the Earl explained briefly.

He sat at the table and glanced round the room.

"Where is Syringa?"

"She retired a little while ago," Lady Elaine replied. "She told us she had a headache, and did not realise it was the oldest and most hoary excuse in the world!"

"An excuse?" the Earl questioned.

"You must not be angry with her, Ancelin," Lady Elaine smiled. "Syringa is young, and like any young girl she is an incurable romantic."

"May I ask what you are talking about?" the Earl enquired in his most uncompromising voice.

"Oh, dear! Have I said too much?" Lady Elaine asked affectedly. "I would not like to betray Syringa's little secret."

"What little secret?"

"Now, Ancelin, you are looking angry," Lady Elaine said.

"Syringa is very young and of course very innocent. She does not realise, I am sure, that she might damage her reputation or indeed annoy you. So you must forgive her and be understanding."

"About what?"

There was a note of thunder in the Earl's voice.

Lady Elaine looked over her shoulder as if she suspected someone might be listening.

"Ninian and I were just wondering who the fortunate gentleman might be," Lady Elaine said softly. "I cannot believe he is someone of whom you would really disapprove, but at the same time it seems strange that she invariably meets him outside the house."

"If you do not make clear to me what you are hinting," the Earl said sharply, "I shall ask my Grandmother for an explanation."

"I am sure she would not be able to give you one," Lady Elaine replied. "I only heard of Syringa's clandestine visits by chance, and of course it was not likely that you would ever learn of them."

"Do you know where she goes?" the Earl asked.

"I have no idea," Lady Elaine answered with a shrug of her shoulders. "But when she makes an excuse to retire early as she did tonight, I know that she creeps out of the house."

She sighed.

"Oh dear! I wish I were young again, young enough to enjoy meeting someone in the shadows! Secret notes, assignations, stolen kisses, oh, how enchanting it used to be!"

Her voice died away as she realised that the Earl was already out of hearing.

He had risen from the table and walking quickly across the room onto the landing was climbing the staircase to the second floor.

Lady Elaine gave a laugh of sheer excitement.

"This is our opportunity, Ninian," she said in a low voice, "we shall never have a better one."

Ninian Roth looked agitated.

"Is everything arranged?"

"Everything!" Lady Elaine replied. "The carriage has been waiting these last two nights. Leave now and do your part. I will see to everything here. Afterwards I shall not sleep at home; His Lordship might try to question me."

"You are certain it is safe?"

"Are you chicken-hearted?" Lady Elaine asked scornfully. "I promise you that if you do not go now it will be too late. I have seen the way he looks at her, and he has not been near me since he has returned to London!"

Her voice was bitter and she continued:

"He will marry her and she will give him half a dozen sons, and you will lose your inheritance. Is that to your liking?"

"No, indeed!" Ninian Roth replied. "But what if you marry him as you wish to do?"

"I have told you before that I cannot have a child," Lady Elaine answered. "Now go and go quickly! You know exactly what to do. It is all a question of timing."

It seemed as if Ninian Roth hesitated for one more moment.

Then he moved quickly across the room to make his farewell to the Dowager.

Syringa came slowly up the back stairs of Rothingham House.

Her feet in their low-heeled satin slippers made no sound on the soft carpet.

With the dark cloak over her shoulders, its hood pulled low, she might have been only a shadow in the flickering light of the guttering candles.

She reached the second floor and paused for a moment before she passed from the servants' quarters into the part of the house occupied by the Quality.

The wall of the great staircase was in front of her and she

noted that most of the candles had been doused in the Hall and there was no sound of voices.

The guests must have gone, she thought, and realised that she was later than usual. She slipped across the landing and opened the door of her bed-room.

As she did so she pulled the heavy cloak from her shoulders and threw it down on the chair just inside the door.

With her hand to her hair, she turned and saw in the light of the candles burning on the dressing table the Earl.

For a moment she was too astonished to speak or to move.

Then as she looked at him she realised she had never before seen a man in such a rage. His face was grim with anger, there was a white line round his mouth and his eyes were as hard as agates.

"So it is true!" he said, and his voice seemed to thunder across the room. "I did not believe what I was told, I thought it impossible! I could not credit that you of all people would deceive me and behave in such a manner. I trusted you, Syringa!"

"I can ... explain ..." Syringa began.

"Do not tell me a pack of lies," he interrupted harshly, "I have no wish to listen to them! I have seen enough! I know now you are like all other women, lustful for the darkness – for someone who is beneath you or who would not gain my approval. Why could you not be honest? Why could you not be frank about it?"

"It is not ..." Syringa cried.

"I believed you to be innocent! I believed you when you said you had no beaux, but I suppose like all other women you have been corrupted by London. God, I have been such a fool! To have thought for one moment that you were as pure as you appeared!"

"No ... no," Syringa cried, "you must ... hear me!"

"What do you want me to hear?" he asked roughly.

Walking towards her he seized her by the shoulders, his

156

fingers biting into the soft skin of her arms.

"Do you think I want to listen to your confessions? Do you think I want to hear you drooling about love? It merely disgusts me – as you disgust me!"

He shook her as he spoke, shook her so she gave a little cry at his roughness.

"I thought you were different!" he said. "I could have taken you and made you mine. After all I had bought and paid for you! But I believed you innocent. God! How could any man be so easily deceived!"

He shook her even harder and then suddenly pulled her close against him, his arms like bands of steel round her trembling body.

"Have you had enough love-making for tonight?" he enquired.

His voice was bitter with mockery. Before she could get her breath to reply he bent his head and his lips were on hers.

He kissed her brutally.

She tried to push him away to save herself from his violence, and then as suddenly as he had taken her, he threw her from him.

"Do you think I want another man's leavings?" he snarled.

She fell against the bed and slipped onto the floor.

"Listen ... please ... listen."

She forced the words between her lips but she was too late.

The Earl, his face contorted into the visage of a devil, looked down at her for one moment, then went from the room slamming the door behind him.

For some seconds Syringa stared after him unable even to cry out, unable to do anything but feel stunned and bewildered by what had happened.

Then slowly she put a trembling hand to her lips, and as she did so, as she felt them bruised and painful to her own touch, she knew that she loved him!

This was love, this streak of fire that had swept through her even as he had held her so roughly in his arms and kissed her so brutally!

It was almost like a blinding light to realise that what she had felt for him all along was not the affection of a friend but the love of a woman for a man!

She loved him! She loved him completely and absolutely, and ... he was incensed with ... her.

She picked herself up from the floor.

"I love ... him," she whispered. "I must go to him ... I must ... explain ... I must tell him that I was not ... doing what he thought."

She gave a little sob. How could he have doubted her? How could he have believed for a moment that she was meeting another man?

"I love him ... I love him."

She found herself repeating the words over and over again just beneath her breath.

She had to find him, she had to tell him now at once that he could still trust her, that she was still all he had believed her to be.

She put her hand to her forehead trying to think. Would he have gone downstairs to the Library or would he have gone to his bed-room?

It would be impossible to visit him there – for whatever would the Dowager say? And yet Syringa knew she could not leave things as they were.

Then as she stood torn by anxiety and irresolute, the door opened.

She looked up eagerly. Perhaps it was the Earl returning – perhaps after all he realised he had been unjust and unkind! But then to her astonishment she saw not the Earl but Lady Elaine.

"Quick, Syringa!" Lady Elaine said in a low voice. "His Lordship wants you at once."

"His Lordship?" There was a lilt in Syringa's tone.

"Yes, hurry, he does not like to be kept waiting."

"No, of course not!"

Lady Elaine looked round and saw the cloak by the door.

"Put on your cloak," she said, "we are going out."

"Out?" Syringa questioned. "Is His Lordship not in the house?"

"No, he wants you to meet him somewhere else," Lady Elaine replied.

"Somewhere else?" Syringa repeated in surprise.

"Ask no questions, he will explain everything," Lady Elaine replied. "Come, we must go."

Surprised but obedient, Syringa let Lady Elaine drape her cloak over her shoulders, then the older woman preceded her out of the door.

"We will go down the back-stairs," she said. "His Lordship's carriage is waiting at the side door."

"But why?" Syringa asked.

"He will explain everything to you," Lady Elaine answered. "Come along, we must hurry."

She led the way along the almost dark passages and down the two flights of stairs which led eventually to the basement.

On the ground floor there was a door leading into Charles Street.

Lady Elaine unlocked it while Syringa stood aside wondering where the Earl had gone and why he wished her to join him.

The door opened and Lady Elaine stepped onto the pavement. Outside there were two coaches.

"Get in," Lady Elaine said as they reached the first one. As there was only a coachman on the box she herself opened the door.

"After you, My Lady," Syringa said politely.

"No, you first," Lady Elaine said insistently and Syringa stepped into the coach.

When she was half way through the door, she felt Lady Elaine give her a hard push which sent her tumbling onto the back seat.

The door was slammed and the horses started forward.

Syringa gave an exclamation realising that she was not alone in the coach. For one moment she thought it might be the Earl.

Then in the dim light of a candle-lantern she saw a Gentleman of Fashion leaning back in the far corner in what she felt was a somewhat negligent attitude.

"Who are you?" she cried, "and why am I here?"

"It is all right, fair charmer," he said and his voice had a cultured tone, "you need not be afraid of me."

"Where are we going?" Syringa demanded. "I was told the Earl of Rothingham wanted me. Are you taking me to him?"

"I regret, most entrancing stranger, at the moment I can convey no information as to our destination."

"Are you a friend of His Lordship?" Syringa insisted.

"Indeed no! To be honest, I have not the honour of His Lordship's acquaintance."

"Then who are you?" Syringa asked.

"As you are interested, my name is Daniel Neame — mostly humbly at your service," the Gentleman replied.

He bowed eloquently from the waist.

"And I am Syringa Melton," Syringa said shyly. "I am sorry to trouble you, Sir, with questions, but I am indeed extremely bewildered."

"You are very young."

Syringa gave a little laugh.

"That is what everyone says to me," she said, "but I shall grow older ... everyone does."

"Yes, alas," Mr. Daniel Neame said with feeling. "When I was your age I felt the world was there for me to plunder. When I was twenty I had my first success on the boards. I felt then that nothing could stop me from reaching the top of my profession."

"On the boards?" Syringa questioned, "do you mean, Sir, that you are an actor?"

"I was one, my dear Lady. No, indeed, I am still one! I

can still play a part, I can still convince an audience that I am who I wish to be."

"Have you played in Shakespeare?" Syringa asked.

"Many times," Mr. Daniel Neame replied. "Once I believed I would be a great Shakespearean actor, but alas I thwarted my own ambitions – thwarted them carelessly and recklessly."

"And how did you do that?"

"Shall I tell you the truth?" he enquired. "There is no reason for us to deceive each other. I drank away my chances and my dreams – as many a better man than I has done."

Syringa thought of her father.

"How sad!" she sighed. "It is such a pity to waste one's life wantonly."

"I agree with you," Mr. Neame said mournfully.

Syringa realised by the tone of his voice that although he was not drunk he had been drinking.

"I am sorry for you, Sir," she said, "but please be kind enough to explain what is happening to me. I think now it was rather foolish of me to believe Lady Elaine when she said the Earl had need of me. I have a feeling ... I may be wrong ... that we are not driving towards His Lordship."

"Lady Elaine?" Mr. Daniel Neame said reflectively. "Is that a lady you have offended? Well, I can understand it. Even in the light of this greasy candle I can see you are very beautiful."

"Thank you, Sir," Syringa said shyly. "But would you be obliging enough to answer my question?"

"I am afraid that is something I cannot do," Mr. Neame replied. "But believe me when I tell you in all sincerity that what I do presently I do with the deepest regret. You are too young, too lovely for the cruelty and the evil of this most unjust world."

There was something in his voice which made Syringa afraid.

"You speak as if something horrible was about to happen to me," she faltered.

"I am afraid so," he said, his voice more melancholy than it had been before, "but there is nothing either of us can do to prevent it."

"I think there is," Syringa replied.

As she spoke she bent forward and put out her hand towards the door.

Mr. Neame made no effort to stop her, and as she felt for it she realised there was no handle.

She turned towards him – a white frightened face.

"I am sorry my dear Lady," he said, "but this is one of those coaches which are used for the abduction of fair maidens! It is also useful to convey from one place to another any who have been enticed to further some nefarious scheme, into the coach in the first place."

"I do not understand what you are ... trying to say," Syringa said, "please ... please ... let me go!"

"Even if I wished to do so, I assure you it is impossible," Mr. Neame replied. "Every precaution has been taken so that you should not escape."

"But why? Where are you taking me, what is all this ... about?"

Syringa had a terrified feeling that she was caught in a trap, that she was being menaced by something so terrifying, so horrible that she could not even put it into thought or words.

"Please, Sir," she said desperately, "tell me what has happened ... or at least give me a chance to get away ... to return to those who ... care for me."

She thought of the Dowager as she spoke and of Nana. Even though the Earl was angry with her, they would help and protect her.

"There is nothing I can do for you, fair charmer," Mr. Neame replied. "I must play my part, and all the world's a stage as far as I am concerned. I have been paid to act and, the actor having accepted a fee, the play must go on. That at least you can understand."

"What part? How am I involved with you in ... this?" Syringa asked.

"You will learn the truth very shortly," he replied.

He drew from his pocket a flask and lifted it to his lips. The smell of brandy seemed to impregnate the whole interior of the coach.

Syringa sank back in her corner trying desperately to puzzle out what was happening, what it could all mean.

Mr. Neame replaced the top of his flask and put it back into his pocket.

She could see now he was older than he had appeared at first. He wore a wig, and she guessed that his face was skilfully made up.

She wondered why even for a moment she had thought him to be a gentleman.

There was something in his bombastic tones which told her all too clearly that he spoke as an actor and declaimed his lines.

She glanced through the closed window. She could see they were passing through dirty narrow streets.

It was very late, but there were still a number of people moving about. Then suddenly the carriage came to a standstill.

They appeared to be in the centre of a small square. The houses surrounding it were dingy with broken windows and the gutters full of filth.

"Why are we stopping here?" Syringa asked apprehensively.

"This is where we alight," Mr. Neame replied.

His voice sounded a little thicker than before, and now as the coach door was opened by the coachman who had descended from the box, he stepped out into the road and with a theatrical gesture reached out his hand towards Syringa.

"Come," he said.

For a moment she thought of refusing to alight.

Then she realised it would be quite easy for Mr. Neame and the coachman to drag her out.

Because she had no alternative she took the actor's hand and stepped from the carriage. Almost immediately the coachman jumped back on the box and drove off.

Syringa looked round her. Even with her dark cloak covering her evening-gown she knew she must look out of place in the poverty-stricken street.

There were men and women in rags and tatters sitting on the steps of the houses and she felt there were eyes everywhere looking at her, watching her.

What light there was came from one lantern and several tarred flares.

There were ragged, barefooted children and a number of rough men of frightening looks standing round a stall selling winkles and whelks. They all turned to stare at Syringa and the Actor.

Suddenly to Syringa's astonishment Mr. Neame drew some articles from his pocket and pressed them into her hands.

"Hold these," he said.

She took them from him automatically then looked down in astonishment. There was a gold watch, a fat purse, a wallet and a tie-pin which glittered in the light.

As she stared at what she held, Mr. Neame began to shout in a loud voice:

"You have stolen my wallet from me! You have picked my pocket! It is an outrage! I shall hand you over to the magistrates! You shall be punished, you are a thief! A thief! A thief!"

His shouts attracted people to converge from the dark corners of every part of the street.

Then as he was still yelling at her, Syringa saw another Gentleman appear. He was dressed as elaborately as Mr. Neame in knee breeches and an evening cloak.

There were two men accompanying him wearing red

waistcoats, and as Syringa glanced up at the sight of them the Gentleman shouted loudly :

"There she is! That is the woman! Seize her! Seize her!"

The two men in red waistcoats ran towards them. Syringa did not move but stood holding in her hands the things which Mr. Neame had given her, her face white and bewildered.

"Seize her!" the Gentleman was saying. "She is a swindler!"

Then to the Bow Street Runners, for that was what Syringa suddenly realised they were, Mr. Neame exclaimed :

"Thank God you have come! Arrest this woman! You can see she holds my watch in her hand, my purse and yes – that is my tie-pin, I have had it for years!"

"It is all a ... mistake," Syringa tried to say, but no-one would listen to her.

The watch and purse were snatched from her. The Bow Street Runners took hold of her arms and hustled her along the roadway.

The people watching began to jeer while the two Gentlemen who had accused her talked loudly, shouting their grievances to each other, repeating over and over again how they had been robbed.

"Please let me ... explain, this is not true...!" Syringa managed to say at least to the Bow Street Runners.

But already they had reached a closed waggon standing a little way along the street.

They hustled her into it so roughly that she fell on the floor, and then the two of them climbed in to sit on the rough wooden seat on either side of the door. There was a rumble of wheels, the voice of a coachman shouting to clear the way.

Syringa, pulling herself onto the seat, realised with horror that she was in a prison waggon!

# Chapter Eight

The Earl returned to Berkeley Square as the sun was rising.

He walked into the house with an expression on his face which made the night-footman glance at him apprehensively.

Placing his cape and hat in the man's hand, the Earl went towards the staircase, but as he was about to ascend it a figure came from the shadows and said:

"May I speak with Your Lordship?"

He glanced round in surprise to see Syringa's nurse standing in the Hall.

"It is very late!" the Earl replied, his hand on the banisters.

"What I have to say is urgent, M'Lord!"

There was a steely note in Nana's voice which the Earl recognised.

Although his inclination was to dismiss her without hearing what she had to say, he turned with an irritated movement of his shoulders and walked across the Hall to the Library.

Nurse followed him and entering the room closed the door behind her.

"What is it?" the Earl asked impatiently. "Surely anything you have to say can wait until the morning?"

"I want to ask Your Lordship," Nana replied, and there was no mistaking the note of defiance in her voice, "what you've done with Miss Syringa."

The Earl made no answer, and after a moment she continued:

"'Tis not right, M'Lord, that she should be taken from this house without my knowledge or without my accompanying her."

"Taken from this house!"

There was no mistaking the astonishment in the Earl's voice as he continued:

"What are you saying? Miss Syringa is upstairs in her room!"

"She's not, M'Lord," Nana contradicted. "If she was, do you imagine I would have waited up for Your Lordship for nearly five hours, hoping for an explanation?"

The Earl stared at Nana as if he could hardly credit what she was saying and then sat down at his desk.

"You tell me that Miss Syringa is not upstairs," he said slowly.

It was as if he found it difficult to articulate the words.

"She was taken away just after one o'clock on Your Lordship's instructions, as I heard with my own ears," Nana retorted.

"Taken away?" the Earl echoed her words.

"That's what I am saying, Your Lordship," Nana replied grimly.

The Earl put his hand to his forehead as if he could hardly take in what was being said.

The wine he had drunk at White's while gambling with a recklessness which had made his friends stare at him in amazement, had left him feeling as if his brain was not functioning properly.

Yet when he spoke again his voice was steady and his eyes watched Nana's face as if he was determined to discover the truth.

"I left Miss Syringa in her bedroom," he said after a moment. "What has happened since?"

"When we came back from the Stables...." Nana began, only to be interrupted by the Earl ejaculating:

"The Stables?"

The words seemed to reverberate round the Library.

167

"Yes, My Lord. Miss Syringa and I had been to Your Lordship's Stables to attend to her horse."

"To attend to her horse?"

The Earl seemed to repeat the words under his breath.

"You were with her?"

"But of course I was with her!" Nana replied sharply. "Does Your Lordship suppose I would let Miss Syringa go out of this house night after night alone? But, M'Lord, you knows as well as I do that she fair dotes on that horse of hers."

"Yes, I know that," the Earl agreed, "but what was wrong? Why should she wish to visit the Stables at that hour of the night?"

Nana hesitated for a moment and the Earl said sternly:

"I want the truth!"

"Very well, My Lord, you shall have it," Nana replied. "Your Lordship's Head Groom is continually at the bottle. He neglects the horses and I shouldn't be surprised if he is selling the feed. 'Tis often enough that they goes short."

The Earl drew a deep breath.

"So Miss Syringa has been out late at night to attend to Mercury."

"That's a fact, My Lord," Nana replied, "seeing that he has enough food and grooming him often as not. I've said to her 'tis not a lady's job, but she'll not listen."

"Why did she not tell me?" the Earl asked.

"I advised she should do so," Nana replied tartly, "but she replied it was not right for her to complain about your Lordship's staff."

"And she met no-one else?"

The Earl asked the question as if he could not prevent it coming from between his lips.

"Who should she meet?" Nana asked. "The grooms were asleep at that time of the night except for those who were out with Your Lordship."

The Earl was silent for a moment. Then he said abruptly:

'What happened tonight?"

"We were later than usual because Miss Syringa thought that Mercury had not been properly groomed," Nana answered. "Brush him down she would although I said she should be between the sheets. Anyway when we came back to the house I went downstairs to the kitchen to get Miss Syringa a glass of milk...."

"So she came upstairs alone," the Earl interrupted.

Again it was as if he spoke to himself.

"As I reached the top of the back stairs," Nana continued as if he had not spoken, "I had the glass of milk in my hand and I was walking careful like as the candles were guttering down low. It was then I heard Your Lordship's voice in Miss Syringa's room. Thinking it best not to interrupt you, M'Lord, I stood in the open door of an empty bedroom."

Pausing a moment she realised that the Earl's eyes were on her face and he was listening intently to every word.

"It was then," Nana said almost dramatically, "that I saw I was not the only person listening."

"What do you mean?" the Earl asked.

"There was someone else the other side of the landing," Nana said, "someone craning foward to hear what Your Lordship was a saying! I could not fail to recognise Her Ladyship with that ruby necklace of hers glittering in the candle-light."

"Lady Elaine was there?" the Earl said almost incredulously.

"She was there and all ears for what was going on," Nana replied with some asperity.

"Continue," the Earl said briefly.

"Your Lordship comes out from Miss Syringa's bedroom, slams the door and goes downstairs," Nana said and there was a reproach in her tone. "I was just about to go in to Miss Syringa, when I thought it might be wise to let Her Ladyship leave first. I knew that Miss Syringa would want no questions asked as to where we'd been so late at night."

"So you waited," the Earl prompted.

"I waited and then to my surprise, Her Ladyship goes in to Miss Syringa. She's only there for a few seconds and then they both comes out with Miss Syringa wearing her cloak."

"Where did they go?" the Earl asked as if he felt Nana's story was needlessly long and drawn out.

"Her Ladyship came out of the bedroom door first. I slipped further into the shadows of the door where I'd been standing, but I heard her say:

" 'We will go down the back-stairs, his Lordship's carriage is waiting at the side door'.

" 'But why?' Miss Syringa asks.

" 'He will explain everything to you,' Her Ladyship replies. 'Come on we must hurry.'

"They passed without seeing me. I put the milk down on the floor and followed them down the back stairs. When they came to the side door that leads into Charles Street, Her Ladyship turns the key and pushes back the bolts.

"They were out on the pavement and the door was closed again before I could get down the last flight of stairs. So I goes to the window and there I sees two coaches."

"Two!" the Earl ejaculated.

"Two," Nana replied, "and I sees Lady Elaine with my own eyes push Miss Syringa into the first. She slams the door behind her, then she stands on the pavement and watches the coach drive away."

"Miss Syringa went alone?" the Earl asked.

"Alone, M'Lord. Then Her Ladyship gets into the other coach which turns round and drives off in the opposite direction."

"I cannot understand it!" the Earl exclaimed.

"Nor can I, M'Lord," Nana replied, "that is why I am asking Your Lordship for an explanation. Where has Miss Syringa gone and why did I not accompany her?"

The Earl rose to his feet.

, "There is something wrong – very wrong."

"But if Your Lordship has no knowledge of my baby's whereabouts," Nana said and now her voice was frightened, "then I'm afeared, desperately afeared that there has been treachery afoot! Miss Syringa expected it."

"Expected treachery?" the Earl exclaimed. "What do you mean?"

"It was when Mr. Ninian Roth and Her Ladyship forced her to sign a paper. They told her it was something to do with fortune-telling, but she says to me when she gets upstairs—

'I did not want to do it, Nana. I had a strange presentiment that they are plotting something evil, something perhaps against His Lordship. I am afraid they may harm him!'"

"When did this happen?" the Earl asked.

Nana considered for a moment.

"It was the evening you gave Miss Syringa the flower brooch. She told me she went into the Salon and Lady Elaine and Mr. Roth were there together."

"What was this paper that she signed?" the Earl asked.

"I don't know, M'Lord," Nana replied. "I wasn't listening to half she said. I only know it perturbed Miss Syringa and she was worried not for herself, but for Your Lordship."

The Earl said nothing and Nana asked plaintively:

"And now what has become of her? If it's treachery, 'tis Miss Syringa who is suffering from it. Find her, M'Lord, and find her quickly, because I feels in my very bones something terrible is a happening!"

"I will find her," the Earl promised and his voice was grim.

"Help me ... God ... help me."

Syringa whispered the words over and over again to herself and felt she was in some terrible nightmare from which she could not awake.

When the great iron-hinged door had swung open, she had known without being told where she was.

There was no need for her to look up at the high gaunt building with its small barred windows, to realise that she had been brought to the most dreaded prison in all London – Newgate.

Then as a half-drunken turnkey, grumbling and using foul language, cursed the Bow Street Runners for wakening him at such an hour, she had heard the shrieking voices of the prisoners echoing and re-echoing round the dark walls. They were like the voices of lost souls.

As Syringa was led along the dark stone passages in the dim light of flickering torches she could see distorted white faces peering at her through bars. Coarse men shouted obscenities at her.

Men were using words of which she did not know the meaning, but which sounded foul and evil.

The fact that a new prisoner had arrived in this loathsome place seemed to arouse a sudden frenzy amongst those who were already imprisoned.

There were shrieks and yells, lewd remarks, and a mocking laughter which followed each raucous sally.

Worst of all there was a terrible stench which made Syringa feel as though she must faint from the very foulness of it!

Mingling with the smell of human excrement, the stink of unwashed bodies and raw spirits, was the smell of fear.

With the Bow Street Runners on either side of her, Syringa followed the turnkey up two flights of stairs. More than once she would have turned and run away blindly and wildly had not the Runners kept their grip on her arms.

Finally on the third floor the turnkey rapped on a locked door which was opened after some minutes by a large blowsy female.

Her body was swollen with drink, her clothes dirty, her hair was hanging untidily on either side of her face beneath a crumpled mob-cap.

"Can't a woman get a bit of sleep in this cursed place?" she enquired truculently.

One of the Runners released his hold on Syringa to draw a guinea from his pocket which he put in the woman's hand. She looked at the coin for a moment, spat on it and said:

"Well that's different! Them that can pay can come at all hours for all I cares!"

"We'll leave 'er with you," the Runner said. "Keep 'er safe."

They turned to leave.

"What's her in for?" the Wardress asked.

"Robbery and swindling," the Runner replied. "Caught with a watch and purse in her very 'ands."

"It is not true!" Syringa cried.

"That's what they all say!" the Wardress snorted. "Ye'll have a chance to prove yerself innocent, if ye can, to the Judge. Don't waste yer lies on me."

She locked the door behind her and walked towards the door of the first cell, through the grating of which a number of faces were watching.

The Wardress took a key from a number hanging from her waist.

"Get along now yer hags," she said to the women peering through the bars, "make way for another thief! Better put yer valuables away."

She laughed coarsely at her joke.

The smell was almost unbearable and Syringa looking inside the cell saw in the not very large room there were over a hundred women and children huddled together. Some of them were sleeping on the floor, some on bare beds with only a rag as a covering.

A number of women had bottles raised to their lips or were already in such a state of drunkenness that they were vomiting on the filthy straw.

They were all of them in a state of dishevelment, half naked and some appeared to have no clothes on at all.

The straw on the floor was thick with excrement. In the far corner some women were cooking, and the smell of grease and oil mingled with human odours made Syringa feel as if she was suffocating.

There were two women near the door in the act of stripping a dead child of its clothes.

They looked up as Syringa stared at them and screamed abuse, though for what reason she could not understand.

Their cries were taken up by other women, and now several reached out their dirty clawlike hands towards Syringa as if they would drag her in amongst them and strip her of her cloak.

They were so menacing that Syringa shrank back against the Wardress as if for protection.

"Frightened?" the woman jeered. "Well ye can pay for better accommodation if ye can afford it."

"I can pay?" Syringa asked.

"If ye have the money," the Wardress replied.

"But I have ... none," Syringa faltered.

"Then there's nothing I can do for ye."

But as the Wardress spoke she looked down at Syringa and saw that her cloak had fallen open as she ascended the stairs and the turquoise brooch with its diamond-centred flowers was glittering on her breast.

"Ye have jewellery," the woman said in a different tone. "I might be able to sell it for ye if ye make it worth me while."

Syringa put her hand over the brooch.

"I cannot do that," she said, "it is not mine, it is only lent to me."

"They'll have it off ye quick enough," the Wardress said roughly, "make no mistake about that."

She gave Syringa a push forward as she spoke as if to fling her in amongst the other women. Their bare arms and dirty hands stretched out towards her.

Syringa gave a little gasp.

"I cannot ... I cannot ... face them, please ... give me a room to ... myself."

The Wardress slammed the cell door and locked it.

"Take off the brooch and let me see it."

With trembling fingers Syringa obeyed her. Even as she

handed it over she wondered distractedly what the Earl would think. His mother's brooch!

The jewel she had promised to return whenever he should ask it of her. And now she was selling it to this fat, dirty woman because she was too afraid to face the occupants of the cell.

But she knew that the Wardress had been right when she said the women would seize it from her the moment she was at their mercy.

"Seven pounds," the Wardress said twisting and turning the brooch in the light from a candle.

"I am sure it is worth ... more than ... that ..." Syringa began and then felt helplessly there was no point in arguing.

"That'll get ye a State apartment," the Wardress said. "Nice and comfortable after this place."

"Then please take me there at once," Syringa said.

She felt she could no longer stand in the passage listening to the foul remarks coming from the women prisoners, hearing their ribald laughter.

One of them was singing a bawdy song and others joined in the chorus shrieking, pointing their fingers as the lewd words were applicable to her.

The Wardress opened the outer door and Syringa followed her back on to the staircase.

Once again she had to run the gauntlet of the men's cells, but by now their rudeness and their obscenity hardly seemed to penetrate her mind.

She was too terrified to think, too numb to be conscious of anything save the fat waddling figure of the Wardress moving ahead of her.

They crossed the courtyard and climbed a flight of wooden stairs to another part of the building. Here it was quieter although there were raised voices behind closed doors.

The Wardress opened the door of a room which seemed to Syringa very dark, dingy and airless, but at least it was empty.

There was a bed with a stained mattress hung with torn curtains in one corner, a threadbare carpet on the floor, a chair and a table.

"Three guineas for the week," the Wardress said, "and seven shillings for the bed."

"Please take the money from what you owe me," Syringa said in a low voice.

She could hardly bear to think of the brooch and what the Earl would say when he knew she had sold it.

"Ye'll have to pay for the three other beds if ye wants it to yerself," the Wardress said. "This be a four-bedded room, and of course I knows that ye would wish to give me a guinea for me trouble. Candles are a shilling, and if ye want a drink ye have to pay for it."

Syringa knew she was being cheated but somehow it did not seem to matter.

"I would like a candle, please."

"And a drink?" the Wardress enquired.

"Nothing, thank you," Syringa said quickly.

"I'll bring ye yer money tomorrow," the Wardress said. "Maybe it'll last ye yer time here."

"What do you mean by that?" Syringa enquired.

"Only that ye're in luck, me fine lady. Ye'll get yer case heard quickly because 'tis the May Sessions at Old Bailey. Some have to wait months before their case be heard, money runs out and they've nought left to sell. Hard on 'em it is!"

"And after I am tried?" Syringa said in a frightened voice, "what will happen then?"

"Ye'll go into the condemned cell," the Wardress replied.

"Condemned!"

Syringa could hardly speak the word.

"For a crime like yer's ye must expect to be hanged! A person stealing anything valued over a shilling gets the gallows. Why a child of three knows that!"

Syringa put her hands up to her neck. She felt that her

voice was constricted in her throat and she could not make a sound.

The Wardress did not seem to expect her to speak. She lit a candle from one in the passage and put it on the table.

Dawn was breaking and a very faint and indistinct light was coming from the glassless window high up on the wall.

"Ye'll get yer money in the morning," the Wardress said, and leaving the cell slammed the door behind her. Syringa heard the key turn in the lock.

For a moment she was unable to move. Then she sat down on the chair and put her face in her hands.

"Help me God ... help me," she prayed, her voice hardly above a whisper.

As she spoke, she saw in the light of the candle a large rat run across the floor and disappear under the bed.

The Court room at Old Bailey was filled with a noisy crowd of people all, it seemed to Syringa, with jeering, hostile ugly faces.

At first with the Judge and Counsel in their white wigs they seemed to swim before her eyes and she thought she was going to faint.

With an effort she held on the wooden railing in front of her and tried to comprehend what was being said.

Her head was aching intolerably and her throat was swollen, so she wondered if when the time came for her to plead she would be able to speak.

She had shivered with cold in her cell when morning brought a chill breeze through the broken window.

Now in the crowded Court Room she felt as if her skin was burning hot and it was hard for her to breathe.

"Ye're lucky," the Wardress had said when she had unlocked the cell door.

Just for a moment Syringa had felt a flicker of hope that she was to be released.

"Yes, lucky!" the woman went on, looking fatter and dirtier than she had the night before. "Two deaths last night and ye're to take the place of one of 'em. It is not often a prisoner is taken to Old Bailey almost before she be settled in so to speak."

"Why did they die?" Syringa asked fearfully.

"Gaol-fever, as ye might expect," the Wardress answered, "twenty-two last month and more the month before. There'll be another epidemic before we knows where we be."

"I am not surprised," Syringa murmured, thinking of the dirt, the stench, the lack of sanitation and the rats.

"Ah, well, we all has to pop off sometime!" the Wardress said, "and it'ld be a pleasure to cheat the Hangman."

She gave a jeering laugh at her own joke.

"Now come along. Ye can tell the Judge ye're innocent and see if he'll believe ye. With a face like yours, ye might even get away with murder, who knows?"

Again she laughed and turned Syringa over to the Turnkey, who escorted her and a number of other miserable prisoners past the cell, through the yards and out through the heavily iron studded door into the waggons which were waiting for them.

In the waggon with Syringa there were three men in chains, one of whom appeared to be completely dazed.

There was a woman who kept muttering about her children who had been left to starve when she had been caught three weeks earlier stealing a loaf of bread with which to feed them.

There was a boy who was a pick-pocket who laughed, joked and said it was his third time in Newgate.

Each time he had come before the Judge he had been able to prove that what he had stolen had only cost eleven pence, and he had therefore escaped the gallows.

There were several others quiet and frightened, dirty dishevelled men and women who seemed too apathetic or too sick to care what happened to them one way or another.

When finally they were taken into the waiting cells at

Old Bailey, it was to find groups of prisoners from other prisons, very much the same mixture, all waiting apprehensively for their cases to be heard.

"I feel so ill I cannot think," Syringa told herself, "but I must be clear headed! I must make them understand this was all a plot!"

A plot contrived by whom? The question had repeated itself in her brain over and over again throughout what remained of the night. Who was responsible?

Had Lady Elaine been acting on the Earl's instructions? Syringa could not believe that, angry though he had been, he would subject her to such degradation or punish her in such a cruel and heartless manner.

Yet he could be ruthless.

She had heard that servants would be dismissed summarily if they did not please him. She knew only too well how harsh he could be, if he did not get his own way.

Nevertheless whatever he was like, whatever he had done to her, she loved him.

"I love him," she whispered, "and now perhaps I shall never see him again ... he will never know that I had done nothing wrong ... nothing of which he could really disapprove."

Last night she had wanted to cry and yet the tears would not come.

Now she felt curiously weak and it was only with the greatest effort that she could prevent herself from sobbing bitterly.

"I must be controlled and restrained," she told herself, "I must make a good impression on the Judge. He must realise that I am a Lady and not a criminal."

How could it all have happened? It all seemed unbelievable, a figment of her imagination.

Lady Elaine escorting her down the back stairs, the Actor waiting for her in the coach, the manner in which he had denounced her, the other Gentleman arriving with the Bow Street Runners and accusing her of swindling him.

It could not be true! It could not have taken place!

Syringa put her hands to her throbbing forehead and with an almost superhuman effort forced herself not to panic, to wait calmly, hoping that she looked composed and that her hair was tidy.

There had of course been no mirror in the cell and she had no comb. She prayed that she did not look like the wildly dishevelled and dirty women who had been brought to trial with her.

There was one who was obviously verminous. She kept scratching her head and her body.

Another was barely decent, her gown had been torn off her breasts perhaps in an effort to take it from her. But it was hard for Syringa to consider anything except the fact that in a few minutes she would be in the dock fighting for her life.

She felt as if she were moving through water, and imagined she saw the silver lake at King's Keep. She was so hot and thirsty that she longed for the coolness of it, but it was no more real than a mirage.

Almost as if someone had struck her and forced her into a realisation of where she was, Syringa saw that Mr. Daniel Neame was in the witness-box.

He was accusing her of stealing his watch, his purse and his wallet.

"Where did you meet this – young woman?"

The Counsel for the Prosecution had a deep voice which seemed always to insinuate far more than what he said in actual words.

"We met in the Argyll Rooms in the Haymarket," Mr. Neame replied. "She was introduced to me by a friend and as she made herself very agreeable, I asked her to supper with me. She appeared quiet and decently behaved, and it was only when I offered to drive her home and we were actually in the carriage that I became suspicious."

"Why were your suspicions aroused?" the Counsel asked.

"I thought her hands were over-familiar," Mr. Neame replied, "and when we arrived at our destination I realised my watch was gone and with it my purse and a wallet containing notes to quite a considerable sum."

"Did you accuse her of theft?" the Counsel asked.

"I did indeed," Mr. Neame replied, "but she laughed at me and would have run away had not at that moment another Gentleman arrived with two Bow Street Runners. I cannot tell you my relief at the sight of them!"

"I can well imagine it," Counsel said.

He turned to the Judge.

"This, My Lord, concerns the second charge against the prisoner. Have I your Lordship's permission to ask the other Gentleman concerned to step into the witness-box?"

"Agreed," the Judge said in a bored tone.

He was a very old man. His face deeply lined, his eye-lids drooped wearily as if he found it extremely tiresome to be present during such long drawn out proceedings.

Mr. Neame stepped down. Now the other Gentleman, whom Syringa had only seen arriving with the Bow Street Runners, was sworn in.

"You know the prisoner?" Counsel asked.

"I do. Her name is Syringa Melton. Some three months ago she was engaged by my aunt, Mrs. Witheringham, to be her companion."

Syringa stared at him in astonishment.

"Your aunt lives in Dorset I believe, Captain Witheringham."

"That is true. She has a large and comfortable house, but she is getting on in years and required a young companion to read to her and to attend to her wishes. Miss Melton seemed at the time an excellent choice."

"Did you become suspicious of her behaviour?"

"I did indeed," Captain Witheringham answered. "I realised Miss Melton was ingratiating herself into my aunt's affections and at the same time poisoning her mind against me as her rightful heir."

"And what did you do about it?"

"I kept a close watch on the young woman. My aunt was getting progressively weaker in health and Miss Melton's hold on her seemed to increase day by day. She persuaded my aunt to give her various trinkets, admittedly not of any great value, but they were undoubtedly jewels and objets d'art which should have gone to her nieces and her nephew."

Captain Witheringham paused dramatically and Syringa realised that he too was an actor.

He was delivering his lines with the same exaggerated sincerity as Mr. Daniel Neame.

"I was shocked and appalled, yes appalled," he continued, "to discover when my aunt fell into a coma that Miss Melton had forged a Will in her own favour."

"You have a copy of this document?" the Judge asked.

"Yes, My Lord," Counsel replied.

Something was passed up to the Judge who perused it for a moment and then said:

"Continue."

"I confronted Miss Melton with the document which Your Lordship has in front of him," Captain Witheringham went on. "She realised that the game was up and that very night slipped away from my aunt's house, taking with her some clothing to which she was not entitled and various other objects which I am quite convinced my aunt had never given her."

"Thank you, Captain," Counsel said. "That, My Lord, concludes the case for the prosecution."

There was a pause while the Judge read his notes, passed a document back to the prosecuting Counsel, then looked towards Syringa.

She tried to clear her swollen throat.

"My Lord . . ." she began.

"You have not taken the oath," the Clerk interposed sharply.

He handed Syringa the Bible and made her repeat the

oath after him. It seemed to her as she spoke that her voice was very weak and frightened.

"I must be calm," she thought, "I have to make them understand."

"Your name is Syringa Melton?"

That the Counsel for the Prosecution's voice now had a bullying note in it was very obvious.

"Yes, Sir."

"I have only two questions to ask you, Miss Melton. The first is, were you or were you not caught by the Bow Street Runners last night with the first witness's gold watch, purse and wallet in your hands?"

"Yes, Sir . . . but I can . . . explain."

"Just answer the question. Yes or no?"

"Y . . . yes."

"My second question," his voice boomed, "is this your hand writing or not?"

He waved a document in front of Syringa's eyes and she saw her own signature in the centre and the name Elizabeth Witheringham in her hand at the end of the paper. There had been a lot of writing added.

She only had time to read the words 'My last Will and Testament . . .' before the Counsel asked again.

"Yes or no? Are the words Syringa Melton and Elizabeth Witheringham in your hand writing?"

"Y-yes," Syringa faltered, "but I am innocent . . . innocent. If I can explain I . . ."

"I submit, My Lord," the Counsel interposed turning to the Judge, "that the prisoner is convicted out of her own mouth. She has admitted, My Lord, to robbery, she has admitted to forgery with attempt to swindle. There is no point, My Lord, in continuing this case and I ask for judgement."

"Very well," the Judge agreed in a bored tone. "Syringa Melton you are found guilty of the crimes of robbery, forgery and an attempt to swindle. For the first crime you are ordered to be hanged by the neck until you are dead.

For the second you shall be stripped naked from the middle upwards and whipped until your body shall be bloody."

"I am ... innocent!" Syringa cried. "Innocent...."

Her voice seemed lost in the noise and chatter that arose in the Court.

Two Warders pulled her roughly from the dock. She was taken down the stairs and hustled towards the door.

As she went she looked at the crowd as if for help or perhaps mercy, and as she did so she saw at the far end of the Court Room a familiar face. It was Ninian Roth!

He was watching her with a smile on his face – a smile of satisfaction. Beside him a Lady, veiled but still recognisable, was smiling too.

It was then, as she had one fleeting glimpse of them before she was pushed through the door and taken to the prison waggon with the other prisoners from Newgate, that Syringa knew who was responsible for all that had happened to her!

Despite her terror and her horror of what lay ahead, she knew that something within herself was glad. Glad because she now knew it was not the Earl who had plotted against her.

As she was rattled back towards Newgate in the swaying waggon, she tried to think coherently of what had occurred. But the headache from which she had been suffering seemed to clamp down on her as if bands of steel were crushing her brain into insensibility.

She could not think, she could not really understand what had happened. How could it be possible that she, Syringa Melton, was to be hanged for a crime she had not committed and whipped until the blood ran down her back?

She remembered now with a kind of sick horror that, as they had been taken through the courtyards of Newgate towards the waggon which would carry them from the prison to Old Bailey, she had seen the Whipping Post erected in the middle courtyard.

She had thought at first it was just the ordinary stocks, such as would be found in every village. And she had wondered why such an old fashioned form of punishment should exist in what was known as the 'new Prison'.

Then she had seen that a couple of iron clasps were fixed to the upright post which supported cross wood to take the culprit's hands and hold him securely while he was being lashed.

The Whipping Post stood in the middle of the yard almost like a cross and Syringa, realising that several of the prisoners looked away from it as they passed, had felt that it was in fact a type of crucifixion.

Now it was to be hers!

She was to stand there, naked above the waist and be lashed with the many tailed whip which she had read about in books. She had learnt that strong men would faint from the pain of it.

"I shall die," she thought, "die under the whipping and perhaps that will be better than dying on the gallows."

They were hustled out of the coach at Newgate and led back the way they had come, the men clanking their chains desperately as they passed through the middle yard and past the Whipping Post.

Syringa saw the women in the party glance at her and knew that she of all the prisoners was the only female who had been sentenced to such a punishment.

They entered the prison amid a chorus of jeers and shrieks and questions concerning their sentences.

Men stretched out their hands towards Syringa making lewd suggestions as how she should spend her remaining time on earth.

The Turnkey took the prisoners to their various cells. Syringa found the Wardress waiting for her and they walked towards the State room she had occupied the night before.

Remembering what the woman had said about being moved to the condemned cell. Syringa asked:

"Can I stay here?"

"No, ye'll have to go with 'em that's condemned," the Wardress replied. "But as ye're to be whipped almost at once, I thought ye would like to let me have yer gown."

"Have my gown?" Syringa questioned in surprise.

"Ye might as well let I have it as the Hangman," the Wardress replied. "'Tis pretty and it'll just about fit me sister's gal. She be only fifteen but it'll make a nice present for her."

Syringa tried to focus her eyes on the fat red face of the Wardress.

She felt a strange buzzing in the head. It was hard to understand what was being said.

"If I part with my gown," she asked, "what shall I wear?"

"They'll have it off ye anyway in the condemned cell," the Wardress said, "besides it be part of the Hangman's perks and he's no friend of mine."

"I want to get a message to the Earl of Rothingham," Syringa said. "I will give you my gown and all the rest of my money if you will carry a note telling him what has happened to me."

The Wardress laughed.

"There bain't no flunkeys here, me fine Lady, to go carryin' notes to Earls or anyone else. If ye wants to get in touch with yer relations ye can ask the Chaplain when he comes to preach the last sermon to ye. That is, if he turns up. He be very irregular in his habits."

"I must send a note to the Earl of Rothingham ... I must." Syringa insisted desperately.

"Ye could ask one of the visitors I suppose," the Wardress said grudgingly, as if she disliked giving the information, "but there's no knowing if they'll carry out yer bidding. Besides why should I give yer good money to throw away on a lot of cheats who'll more than likely spend it on drink."

"Please ... please try and get in touch with the Earl,"

Syringa begged. "I know he will reward handsomely any-one who tells him where I am."

The Wardress gave an ugly laugh.

"Do ye really expect me to believe ye?" she asked. "I expect that's as good a lie as yer telling me ye were inno-cent. Ye haven't been able to prove that in the Courts, have ye? Well, I'm not one to be gulled easily. I've been here too long.

"Come on now, give me yer gown. I've got more use for it than ye and the money I still has for ye simply because I'm honest, ye can spend on gin. They say if ye're drunk enough ye don't feel the noose."

Syringa stood irresolute. Roughly the Wardress turned her round and started unbuttoning her gown at the back.

There was something about the woman's thick dirty fingers touching her bare skin that made her want to scream.

"Perhaps I shall ... die," she said speaking to herself.

"No, they don't kill ye," the Wardress said. "They beat ye until ye're insensible, then carry ye back and throw ye on the ground at me feet. Extra work this whipping busi-ness gives me, I can tell ye."

She had undone Syringa's gown by now and began to pull it from her shoulders.

It was one of the pretty gauze gowns that the Dowager had bought from Madame Bertin. The skirt was edged with pleated frills of tulle and there was tulle around the shoul-ders.

The waist was very small and embellished with pale tur-quoise blue satin that had matched the stones in her flower brooch.

The gown slipped to the floor and now Syringa wore only the silk petticoats which had kept the gown full, and over her breasts a thin muslin shift edged with lace.

It was transparent and feeling naked she crossed her hands over her breasts. The Wardress looked at her shift appreciatively.

"They'll pull that down when they whip ye, dear," she said. "Don't let them splatter it with too much blood, I'd like to have that too when ye've gone."

Syringa closed her eyes. There seemed no point in arguing.

"They'll be fetching ye soon," the Wardress said putting her gown over her arm. "T'may be an hour, t'may be more. What I always say is, the sooner the better. Thinking about a whipping be almost as bad as having it."

She went from the cell. For a moment Syringa stood holding onto the table as if for support.

Then she fell on her knees and started to pray.

Her head felt as though it was bursting open. The pain was almost unbearable. Her whole body ached intolerably and now the glands in her neck were so swollen she felt as if her breath was constricted.

Yet she knew she must pray. At this moment only prayer could help her.

"I must pray to be ... brave," she told herself. "How degrading ... how humiliating if I scream ... cry and beg for ... mercy ... mercy I know I shall not ... receive. I must be ... brave ... I must!"

And yet in front of her eyes she could see only the Whipping Post, its arms standing out like a cross in the centre of the yard.

"Help me ... oh God ... help me!"

Her lips moved but there was no sound.

"Help me to be brave ... help me to face what lies ... ahead ... help me not to ... scream."

She thought of the Earl and knew that in such circumstances he would be brave.

His pride would not let him humble himself. The mere thought of him seemed to bring some solace to her fear.

"I love ... him," she told herself, "I love ... him!"

Then in an agony which seemed to come from the very depths of her being she prayed.

"Oh God ... let him ... save me ... Save me, Lord Jupiter! ... Save me!"

Even as she whispered the words inaudibly, she heard the key turn in the lock of the cell and there was the sound of men's voices. They had come for her!

They had come to take her outside to the Whipping Post and she knew that nothing now could save her!

The door was open, someone was standing inside. Fearful she opened her eyes and saw in the doorway – the Earl.

Somehow she scrambled to her feet and tried to cry out her joy at the sight of him, but the sound would not come.

Then as she struggled towards him the darkness seemed to come up from the floor and envelop her.

As the Earl caught her in his arms, he thought for one agonising moment that she was dead.

# Chapter Nine

Everything was very dark.

Somewhere far away in a long endless tunnel a woman was crying aloud, her voice weak and piteous, but persistent.

"Help me ... Oh God help me ... send him to save me ... I am to be hanged by the neck until I am dead ... hanged by the neck ... they are going to whip me ... I must not cry ... I must be brave as he would be brave ... I must not scream ... they will whip me until the ... blood flows ... Oh God save me ... Jupiter ... Lord Jupiter!

"He is angry with me ... he will not come ... how could he think such things of me ... when I love him ... I love him ... he is angry ... he does not understand. Save me! ... they are clutching at me ... I am afraid of their hands ... save me ... save me..."

"You are safe!" a deep voice was speaking. "Do you hear me, Syringa, you are safe."

"He does not ... understand ... he does not know that ... I love him..."

"He knows and he understands. Go to sleep, Syringa, go to sleep."

"Well, Miss Melton, there is nothing more I can do for you!"

Dr. Gresham stood by the bedside looking down at Syringa. She had known him since she was a child and she had always sent for him when her father was beyond her control.

"I can go downstairs?"

"Whenever you wish. You are quite well again."

"I have been well for days."

"We had to be quite certain," the Doctor replied. "There is always the fear of a relapse, and then you might carry the infection to other people."

"Yes, I realise that."

"But your Nurse tells me you have been very sensible. You have walked about the room. You have done exercises so that now when you are allowed out into the fresh air, you should not feel unnaturally fatigued."

"All I want to do," Syringa said with a smile, "is to ride Mercury."

"I expect you will find him waiting for you," Dr. Gresham said. "Send for me if I am needed, but I do not expect to hear from you."

"Goodbye Doctor, and thank you."

Nana showed the Doctor to the door. As it shut behind him Syringa sat up in bed.

"I can get up! I can go out!" she cried. "Oh, Nana, if you only knew how much I have been looking forward to seeing Mercury again!"

"Now wait a minute, Miss Syringa," Nana said, "His Lordship has given me his instructions."

"His Lordship?"

Syringa said the words almost beneath her breath and then she added:

"He is ... here?"

"Of course His Lordship is here!" Nana replied. "He has been here all the time, ever since you have been ill."

"I had no idea," Syringa answered.

She did not tell Nana that she had been afraid to ask for the Earl.

When she came back to consciousness from a delirium which she knew now had lasted for weeks, she had remembered that the Earl had been angry with her. And she was afraid, as she had never been afraid before, of seeing him again.

Her first thought, when she had realised that she was at King's Keep and still alive, had been of him.

But in her weakness she had known that she could not face his anger, could not endure it if he was still incensed with her as he had been that terrible night when Lady Elaine had sent her to Newgate Prison.

Her love of him made her so apprehensive that she could not bring herself to speak of the Earl to Nana, in case the answers to her questions were unbearable.

Supposing he never wished to see her again?

He had said that she disgusted him. He would know now, because Nana would have told him, that she had not been meeting a man as he had suspected!

But had he still any fondness for her?

He loved Lady Elaine. Would his feelings change if he learnt of her cruelty and treachery? Perhaps there would be no-one to tell him and he would never know.

Then Syringa's heart dropped and she thought miserably that even if the Earl became aware of the truth, he would forgive Lady Elaine if he loved her enough.

"What are His Lordship's ... instructions?" she asked Nana.

"His Lordship wishes you to go downstairs at six o'clock," Nana replied. "Until then he asks that you should rest."

"I am tired of resting," Syringa protested. "I have been resting for days even though I have felt well enough to go out."

"We have had to take great care of you, dearie," Nana said. "You have been very ill – very ill indeed."

"And Gaol Fever is often fatal," Syringa sighed. "I am lucky, am I not, Nana? Men and women die of it every day in that horrible prison."

"Do not speak of that wicked place!" Nana said with a suspicion of a sob in her voice. "His Lordship has said it is all to be forgotten."

"It will not be ... easy to ... forget," Syringa murmured.

"I know, dearie," Nana answered, "but now you are well again, you will have other things to think about."

"What other things?" Syringa asked. "And what are we going to do in the future, Nana, you and I?"

"You must ask His Lordship," Nana replied evasively. "All I know is that he wishes you to rest and then go downstairs to see him at six o'clock, wearing a new gown he specially ordered for you."

"A new gown from His Lordship!" Syringa exclaimed with a little lilt in her voice. "How kind of him. Did you bring all my others down from London?"

"They are all here," Nana replied.

Syringa looked round the great room, so impressive with its embroidered curtains and carved gilt mirrors.

It was the most beautiful of all the State Bedrooms at King's Keep.

The great bed had a canopy surmounted by doves and the coral silk draperies were caught to the wall with gold angels.

"I suppose my clothes are in the bedroom I had before I went to London," she said.

"That was where His Lordship took you when you first arrived," Nana said. "Now it has been disinfected. Everything, the curtains, the bed hangings, the linen were all burnt."

"Burnt!" Syringa exclaimed.

"Gaol Fever is very infectious, dearie. His Lordship was taking no chances. The interior of the coach in which we brought you here was washed down with vinegar."

"And nobody caught the fever from me?" Syringa asked anxiously.

"No-one came near you," Nana replied. "Only His Lordship and I attended you."

"His ... Lordship?"

"He nursed you, Miss Syringa. We took it turn and turn about. His Lordship at night and I in the day time."

"I had no ... idea," Syringa said in a low voice.

Yet she thought she must have known he was there even when she was delirious.

Someone had soothed her, someone had told her she was safe and must go to sleep. She had thought it was all part of her frightening dreams.

Dreams when she believed they were coming to hang her, when she was about to be whipped, and the obscene creatures in the cells reached out their clutching hands towards her and she could not escape! She had been afraid – desperately afraid.

She could remember now a woman screaming – it must have been herself.

Then strong arms had held her, an authoritative voice had commanded her to forget her fears.

Feeling embarrassed at the thought of the Earl having seen her in such a state, she asked hesitantly:

"How did His Lordship ... know what to ... do? How could he know ... anything ... about ... nursing?"

"His Lordship said he had nursed people with fevers in India," Nana replied. "Very competent he was, and only he could soothe you when you were in such a high fever that we thought you must die. Gaol Fever is a terrible illness, my dearie. I hopes never to see it again in the whole of my life."

"Do I ... look ugly?" Syringa asked.

Her eyes were so anxious that Nana fetched her a hand-mirror from the dressing-table and Syringa stared at her own reflection.

She was thinner, so that her eyes seemed to fill her whole face; but her hair was still curling luxuriantly back from her white forehead and her skin was unblemished.

"Perhaps he will notice no difference in me," she thought to herself.

Because she wanted so desperately to look nice for the Earl, she made no protest as Nana drew the curtains but lay back against the pillows and shut her eyes.

It was a hot day and she needed only a linen sheet to cover her.

But it was not like the blistering heat she had endured with the fever when at times she had felt that she must be burning in the fires of hell.

What did the Earl think of her, she wondered as she had screamed and cried. Had he only a contempt for her because she was a coward?

She hoped she had not said too much while she was unconscious. How humiliating it would be if she had revealed her love for him!

She winced but she was fearful too of broaching the question she longed to ask him. What should she say if he questioned her to find out who had been responsible for her arrest.

It must have been Lady Elaine and Ninian Roth who had instructed and paid the actors to give false evidence against her and who had got the signature to the contrived Will.

But how could she tell the Earl such things without any positive proof? How could she accuse his cousin and the woman he loved of such perfidy?

There were so many problems ahead.

While every nerve in her body longed to see him, her mind shrank from the inevitability of what must be said if they discussed what had happened.

Yet when Nana called her at half past five, brought her a bath scented with rose petals, and started to dress her in her gown, Syringa felt an irrepressible excitement which overrode her fears.

The gown was of white gauze and with an undertone of silver in the full skirts which made it shimmer like moonlight as she moved.

There was soft tulle to frame the whiteness of her neck and cover her shoulders.

Again there was that shimmer of silver which made Syringa look as though she were a sprite arising from one of the iridescent fountains playing in the garden.

"It is a lovely gown, Nana!" she exclaimed.

"It really needs a brooch in the front of it," Nana replied.

Syringa felt her heart miss a beat as she remembered that she must tell the Earl what had happened to the brooch he had lent her – the brooch which had belonged to his mother and which she had sold in Newgate Prison.

Nana had brushed Syringa's hair until it seemed to have new lights in it, lights which echoed the silver in her gown.

Then she brought from a side-table a little wreath of wild flowers.

There were daisies, periwinkles, wild rose-buds and honey-suckle all entwined together, their fragrance very subtle and sweet.

"How pretty!" Syringa cried.

"His Lordship sent it for you," Nana replied. "I can't think why he should worry with wild flowers when the green-houses are full."

Syringa said nothing.

She felt the wreath had a special message for her, and yet she was afraid to guess at it, afraid to put it into words even to herself.

Ready, she rose to her feet and looked at herself in the long mirror.

"You are very beautiful, my dearie!" Nana said.

Syringa heard a sob in her voice and saw the tears in her eyes.

"I am well, that is more important than anything else, Nana," Syringa smiled, "and I must thank you for it."

"And His Lordship! Don't forget to thank His Lordship!"

"I will thank him."

Syringa reached the door and looked back.

"You are not unhappy, Nana?" she asked.

"No, I am happy, Miss Syringa. Happy for you! Good luck, my baby."

Syringa looked a little surprised and then she supposed her illness had made Nana over-emotional.

"All the same," she thought to herself as she went slowly down the staircase, "I need luck."

196

She needed it because she was to see the Earl again and she prayed that he was no longer angry with her.

To her surprise the great Hall was empty.

The front door was open letting in the warm golden July sunshine, but there were no footmen in attendance, no Meadstone to lead her pompously towards the Library where she knew instinctively the Earl would be waiting for her.

She crossed the Hall slowly, feeling suddenly small and insignificant.

Her heelless slippers made little sound on the marble floor. When she reached the Library door she hesitated a moment.

She wanted to see the Earl, she wanted so much to be with him, but she knew it was going to be hard not to reveal her gladness and her love.

Things must now be different between them, she thought.

She had loved him before it was true, but without realising it. What was love she had believed to be friendship.

Now the truth made her inexplicably shy and yet overwhelmingly excited.

She turned the handle of the door and entered.

The room was bathed in the afternoon sunshine and fragrant with the scent of the roses arrayed in great bowls on nearly every table.

The Earl was standing looking out of the window. As she entered he turned towards her and she saw him against a background of glory.

She had forgotten, she thought, how tall, broad-shouldered and overwhelming he was.

Because her heart turning a somersault was beating violently in her breast, she found herself unable to speak, unable to move.

"Syringa!"

His voice was very deep and there seemed to be a note in it she had never heard before.

He walked towards her and with an almost superhuman

effort she forced herself not to run to his side, but to move slowly and deliberately.

"You are well?"

She looked up at him, and at the expression on his face her eyelashes fluttered to lie dark against the pallor of her cheeks.

"Come and sit in the window," he suggested.

Obediently she walked towards the wide satin-cushioned window-seat.

The casements were open and the sunshine was warm against her pale cheeks and on her bent head.

"There is so much we have to say to each other, Syringa," the Earl said quietly.

He had seated himself beside her but somehow she dared not look up at him.

"I have to ... thank Your Lordship ... for nursing me," Syringa began in a low voice. "I am distressed ... that I was such a trouble to you."

"You were certainly the cause of much anxiety," the Earl replied.

"I am ... sorry."

"There is no need."

"But you should have been in London with the ... Prince and your ... friends."

"Do you think they were important when I was indirectly responsible for your illness?"

There was something in the Earl's tone which made Syringa feel it was hard to breathe.

"How did ... you ... find me?" she managed to say in a tight little voice.

"When your nurse told me Lady Elaine had taken you downstairs and put you into a coach, I went straight to her house," he replied. "She was not there and her butler had no idea where she might be."

He paused as if remembering his frustration.

"I then repaired to Ninian's lodgings. To my surprise, although it was only a little after eight o'clock, he had already left. His man-servant disclaimed any knowledge of what his destination might be, but after some encouragement he suggested that his Master might be with his theatrical friends."

Syringa raised her head a little.

"After further questioning," the Earl went on, "I ascertained that during the past week Ninian had on several occasions entertained two actors at his lodgings. The manservant, from scraps of conversation he had overheard, thought they were rehearsing a play in which a Court Room was involved."

The Earl's voice was harsh as he continued:

"My suspicions were already aroused because your Nurse had told me of a paper which Ninian and Lady Elaine had persuaded you to sign. When I found in my cousin's desk some rough copies of a Will, I left immediately for Old Bailey."

"So that is how ... you found out what had ... happened."

Syringa hardly seemed to breathe the words.

"When I reached the Courts I learnt that the case was over," the Earl said, "and you had already been taken back to Newgate."

Syringa made a convulsive gesture as if his words brought back the horror and misery of hearing herself sentenced.

"Do not let us speak of it any more," the Earl said quickly. "It is over and you are safe. There are more important matters to discuss."

His voice altered.

"First of all, I want to apologise. To tell you I am most sincerely repentant and to beg your forgiveness."

She knew of what he spoke. It was no use pretending she did not understand.

"How ... how could you think such ... things of ... me?"

"I have asked myself that a thousand times," he replied.

"I was crazy to imagine for one moment you were not what you appeared to be."

"Nana told you that we went to the Stables to see Mercury?"

"She told me," the Earl replied. "The groom has been dismissed, but, Syringa, I blame myself for not taking better care of my own horses."

"Mercury is ... all right?"

"He is here waiting for you to see him."

"I hoped that you would have brought him to King's Keep from London as you ... brought me."

"I thought that both you and Mercury would do better in the country," the Earl said. "He has been exercised every day, but it is not the same as having his mistress on his back."

"Perhaps I could ride him ... tomorrow."

"Of course, if you wish to do so."

Syringa's eyes were still downcast.

"There is ... something I wish to ... say to Your Lordship," she said after a moment.

"I am listening," the Earl answered quietly.

"You may think it very ... stupid of me," Syringa faltered, "but I could ... not go ... back to ... London."

There was a moment's pause and Syringa held her breath in case he should be angry.

"I can understand why you are feeling like that," he said, "and I promise that you shall not go back to London until you wish to do so. But there is no need for you to feel afraid."

"Why?" she enquired.

"Because," the Earl answered, "my cousin Ninian and Lady Elaine are no longer in London. They have left the country."

There was steel in his voice and the words sounded harsh and formidable.

"Why ... have they gone?" Syringa asked nervously.

"I gave them the choice," the Earl replied, "of leaving the

country for the rest of their lives or standing trial. Knowing only too well the penalty for an attempt at swindling, they not unnaturally chose to go abroad."

"I was ... afraid," Syringa said hesitatingly, "that it would ... upset you to know what ... Lady Elaine had ... done."

"What upset me was that cruelly and criminally she had made you suffer. That is something which I will never forgive."

There was a ruthlessness in his tone which made Syringa clasp her fingers together.

"My feelings for Lady Elaine need not concern us," the Earl said. "In effect she no longer exists. Had you anything else to ask me?"

"If I need not go back ... to London," Syringa began hesitatingly, "I wonder whether Your Lordship would permit ... Nana and me to ... live in a ... small cottage here on the ... Estate?"

She looked up at him anxiously as she spoke, hoping he would not think she was imposing on his generosity.

"And do you think you would be content in a small cottage?" he asked, his eyes watching her face.

"Perhaps I c-could ... see y-you ... s-sometimes," Syringa stammered.

"And would that be enough," the Earl asked, "for you or – for me?"

She did not understand what he was saying, and because the tone of his voice made her feel suddenly very shy she said quickly:

"There is ... something else I have to ... say to Your Lordship, something that I should have said ... at once."

"And what is that?" he asked.

"You have apologised to me," she said, "but it is for ... me to apologise to ... you most ... humbly and ... abjectly. I want to ask you ... forgiveness and yet I do not ... know how to do so."

"For what?" the Earl enquired.

"For ... selling the brooch that you ... lent me," Syringa replied miserably. "I have thought about it ... ever since I have been ... here and I am so ... utterly and completely ... ashamed that I was so ... dishonest and so ... cowardly. But I could not face ... those women. They were like ... animals, and when they put out their ... hands towards ... me I thought if they ... touched me I should go ... mad."

Her voice broke.

Then the Earl's hands were on hers as she twisted her fingers together on her lap. She felt the warm strength of them and found herself quivering at his touch.

"You are not to talk about it," he said, "you are to forget what you have suffered. It is over, Syringa. It is an experience through which you should never have passed and I have cursed those who inflicted it upon you. But now you are to erase it from your mind. Do you understand?"

"I will ... try," Syringa said humbly, "if you will ... forgive me."

"There is nothing to forgive," the Earl answered.

"You do not ... despise ... me?"

He could hardly hear the words.

"I admire you for your courage, Syringa, and I think you are braver than any other woman I have ever known."

Syringa drew in her breath and her eyes went to the Earl's face as if she could hardly believe what he had said.

He looked down at her and she felt something quiver and come alive within her heart.

"I was ... not really ... brave," she said. "I was ... terrified ... and I could only pray ... for you."

"For me?"

"To save ... me ... I thought God ... would send ... you."

"He did send me."

"If you ... had ... not ... come ... in time ..."

"Forget it!" the Earl's voice was sharp. "You are here, safe, and we are together."

"To . . . gether!" Syringa hardly breathed the word.

"I have something to show you."

As the Earl spoke he rose, drew Syringa to her feet, and holding her hand in his led her across the room to his desk.

She wondered what he wanted her to see, then saw, lying on the crimson velvet blotter emblazoned with the Roth Coat of Arms, something which glittered in the sunshine. It was the turquoise brooch.

Syringa gave a cry of sheer delight.

"You have it back! Oh I am so glad! So very glad! It has worried me . . . desperately that you should have lost something so precious to you."

"I bought it back for you," the Earl said.

He picked it up as he spoke, staring down at it as if he had never seen it before.

"Tell me, Syringa," he said after a moment, "do you remember why my mother gave this brooch to me?"

"Yes, of course," Syringa replied, "she gave it to you for your wife."

"And that is why," the Earl said very quietly, "I am asking you now, Syringa, to accept it as – a gift."

It seemed to Syringa that her heart stood still. Then in a small frightened voice she said:

"I do not think I . . . understand what you are . . . saying."

"I will try to make it clearer," the Earl answered. "I love you, my darling, and I want, more then I have ever wanted anything in my life, that you should marry me."

Syringa looked up at him. She was trembling and her grey eyes searched his face as if she thought she could not have heard him correctly.

Very gently he put his arms round her.

"I love you," he said, "and I think, although I may be mistaken, that you love me."

"Did I . . . tell you . . . so?" Syringa whispered.

"You told someone called Jupiter that you loved him,"

the Earl answered, "and I believed I was linked in your poor tortured unhappy little mind with the god after whom you had so flatteringly nick-named me."

His arms tightened about her.

"God or no god – do you love me enough to marry me, Syringa?"

"You are so ... important ... of such ... consequence," Syringa said. "I should be overwhelmingly happy just to be with you ... and to know that you ... cared for me ... a little."

The Earl's arms tightened about her so that she could hardly breathe.

"Do you think my love for you is little?" he asked. "Do you think I would ever risk losing you again? My foolish darling, although I did not realise it, I have been seeking for you all my life. You will always be with me, safe and in my arms now and for ever, because you are my love, the woman I worship and my wife."

He pulled her closer as he spoke and slowly and very gently his lips sought hers.

He kissed her as he had done the first time in the wood as if she was a child he was afraid he might hurt.

Then as he felt her lips cling to his and a quiver of excitement run through her, so that she trembled but not with fear, his mouth became more insistent, more possessive.

To Syringa it was as if the whole world was golden and the wonder of it was too intense to be borne.

She felt an ecstasy such as she had never known before and she knew that this was what she too had been seeking and they were one, a man and woman who had found each other and were complete.

The Earl raised his head and looked down at her eyes shining as if they were stars.

"I love you ... Oh Lord Jupiter ... I love ... you," she whispered brokenly and hid her face against his shoulder.

He kissed her hair.

"Come, darling."

She felt him take his arms from her and looked up in surprise.

"Where are we going?"

"It is a secret, I want you to trust me."

"You know ... I do that."

"You are so lovely, so perfect," he said and his voice was hoarse.

Then, with an obvious effort, he took her hand and drawing her along beside him he turned towards the door.

The Hall was still empty, and although Syringa wondered at the lack of attentive flunkeys, she had not time to mention it.

The Earl led her through the sunlit door. Standing below the steps was a familiar figure.

It was Mercury tossing his head and whisking his tail to keep away the flies.

To Syringa's astonishment he was harnessed to a small curricle which was gaily decorated with flowers and ribbons.

She ran down the steps.

"Mercury! Mercury!" she cried. "How I have missed you!"

The great horse whinnied and nuzzled his nose against her.

"You have taught him to pull a curricle!" Syringa said to the Earl, her face alight as she patted Mercury's neck.

"I have taught him to obey me as he obeys you. Now he has somewhere to take us."

He helped Syringa into the curricle, arranging her full skirts and then seated himself beside her. As he picked up the reins, Syringa laid her face against his arm.

"I am so ... happy," she murmured.

"If you look at me like that," the Earl warned her, "I shall find the greatest difficulty in driving."

Syringa gave a little laugh of sheer joy.

As Mercury took them down the drive at a steady trot, she wondered where they were going.

They soon left the avenue of oak trees and set off across the park on a grass track which led towards the woods. Syringa's eyes widened but she asked no questions.

When they reached Monk's Wood she saw there was a new track just wide enough to take the curricle, winding between the pine trees and going deep into the heart of the wood.

It was not hard now to guess where they were going, and when finally Mercury came to a halt beside the thick thorn hedge, Syringa looked up at the Earl.

He put down the reins and she thought he would take her in his arms, but instead he alighted and came round to her side of the curricle to help her out.

He went ahead of her and she followed him, realising that he moved without faltering through the thorn hedge as she had done the first time that she had led him there.

When they stepped together into the secret place, the Earl took her hand and held it very tightly while she looked round.

The grass was a carpet of white daisies, golden buttercups and blue periwinkles, beside the fallen masonry were great clumps of crimson poppies.

The thorn hedge was verdant green and the wall of shrubs which surrounded the Chapel and made a screen for the altar had burst into flower.

There were pink dog-roses, yellow honeysuckle, mauve and white convolvulus growing over the grey stones and a dozen other flowers all adding their colour and their beauty to the sanctuary.

Against the Altar standing waiting for them was a man in white.

He was standing so still that Syringa thought for a moment that he must be an illusion.

Then as she looked enquiringly at the Earl he said softly :

"Where else could we be married, my darling, but here?"

Her fingers tightened on his and they moved towards the Priest.

The song of the birds was like some angelic choir.

Everywhere in the shrubs and the trees, beneath the fallen stone work, Syringa felt the little eyes of the forest creatures were watching them.

When they reached the Altar she and the Earl knelt down on the moss-covered steps and the Priest started the marriage service.

Syringa heard the Earl's voice, firm and steady, make the marriage vows and she repeated hers softly but with a sincerity which came from the very depths of her heart.

Her fingers trembled a little as the Earl put the ring on her finger and then she shut her eyes to receive the blessing.

The Priest made the sign of the cross then he laid one hand on Syringa's head and the other on the head of the Earl as he finished.

"... And the blessing of God Almighty, the Father, the Son and the Holy Ghost, be with you both now and for ever more."

It seemed to Syringa that as he spoke everything was very quiet.

Then as his voice ceased the birds filled the wood with song. There were the notes of the blackbirds, the chaffinch and the wrens, the coo of the wood-pigeon, the hoot of an owl, the caw of the rooks.

It was like a paean of praise going up to Heaven.

As she prayed that her love would never fail the Earl and that they would belong to each other for all eternity, she felt him very gently draw her to her feet.

They were alone.

The Priest had vanished, almost as if their marriage had been a divine visitation and not a human ceremony.

"My wife!" the Earl said the words very softly.

Then he kissed her as he had kissed her once before on her forehead. There was something so spiritual and dedicated in the gesture that Syringa felt the tears come to her eyes – tears of happiness and of love.

Without speaking again the Earl led her back over the

grass and through the thorn hedge to where Mercury was waiting for them.

In silence they got into the curricle and drove back through the trees of Monk's Wood and out into the park again.

The sun was sinking low, the sky was crimson and gold, King's Keep was exquisitely beautiful – a jewel in a green velvet setting.

To Syringa's surprise they did not drive straight to the house. Mercury went along the narrow track leading behind it towards one of the hills.

Only as they started the climb so that the house lay beneath them, did Syringa realise that ahead, silhouetted against the setting sun was the great Observatory which had been built by the Earl's grandfather.

She wondered why they were going there but she asked no questions. She was content to lay her cheek against his arm as she had done when they left King's Keep.

She was vividly conscious of the narrow gold band encircling the third finger on her left hand.

She thought that only the Earl could have planned that they should be married in their Secret Place. A place she knew now where she must first have fallen in love with him.

Higher and higher Mercury climbed until finally he drew up outside the pillared front of the Observatory.

Syringa looked it in surprise.

"I thought it was derelict and unsafe," she said. "The Colonel would never allow me to come here."

"Your Italian friends have been working here all the time you were ill," the Earl explained with a smile. "Come and see what they have done."

He knotted the reins together as he spoke and attached them to the box of the curricle.

Then having assisted Syringa to alight he said to Mercury:

"Go home, Mercury – go home!"

To Syringa's amazement the horse that formerly had obeyed only her turned round slowly and carefully and obediently started back down the hill.

"Will he really go home for you?" Syringa asked.

"We have rehearsed this many times," the Earl answered, "and he has never failed yet to turn up at the stables where the grooms are waiting for him."

"And how shall we get home?" Syringa enquired.

"Are you in such a hurry to leave?" the Earl asked.

She thought she had never seen him look so happy or so young.

He led her through the newly painted door and when she was inside she gave a gasp.

The Observatory had been built originally in the shape of a Roman temple. There were high pillars, alcoves containing marble statues, and the floor was of exquisite tiles. The windows, and there were many of them, were open to the light of the setting sun.

On the walls which had now been restored were painted murals. Pictures of Venice, the cypress trees of Florence and the ruins on the Appian Way.

The whole room was decorated with shrubs. There were green plants of every sort and description.

Plants, ferns and ivy, and yet the eyes seemed inevitably led towards the windows with their breath-taking view.

The Earl led her to one and Syringa realised they were looking for miles over the countryside, as they had done that first day when they had met, when she had taken him to 'the look out'.

"I understand," she said slowly, "I understand ... now what you have been telling me ever ... since I left my ... bedroom. This is 'the empty world' ... yours and mine ... that is why we have seen no-one and just been ... alone."

"Our empty world," the Earl said, "a world through which you and I can tread our path together. Together, darling, towards the horizon."

"No-one else but you could say ... anything like that ...

or think of anything that could make me so ... happy," Syringa cried.

"It is you who have taught me to understand such things," he said.

He took her in his arms and his lips found hers.

He kissed her until her breath came quickly between her lips and then while she still longed for him to hold her even closer, he said:

"I do not wish to tire you. Come and sit down and have something to eat and drink. It is your first day out and I must be very considerate."

"I am not tired," Syringa protested.

"The evening is not yet over," he replied. "There are still some surprises left."

She let him lead her to a table which she had not noticed before set on the other side of the room.

On the white table cloth on the sideboard there was every sort of delicacy and bottles of wine resting in a huge crested silver ice-cooler.

The Earl poured the golden wine into two crystal glasses and then raised his towards Syringa.

"To my wife," he said.

"To my ... husband," Syringa replied softly.

"And to our love," the Earl said.

They drank and then laughing almost like children they enjoyed their dinner together.

The Earl waited on Syringa and kissed her between every course so she found it hard to realise what she was eating and felt that everything tasted like ambrosia.

When they had finished the Earl sat back in his chair a glass of brandy in his hand, his eyes on Syringa.

Her little face was flushed and radiant in the light of the candles.

"Were the Italians pleased to be able to work here again?" she asked.

"They laboured day and night to get it finished," the Earl answered, "and they achieved the impossible in so short a time. They even restored the mosaic bath which was brought here from Rome."

"How could they do so much so quickly?" Syringa asked.

"I told them it was for you," the Earl replied. "I have often wondered if the workmen ever slept at all! They are very grateful to you, Syringa."

"And to you," Syringa said quickly.

"You will have to teach me to understand my people," the Earl said.

"I do not think really you need any teaching," she answered. "I have never met anyone who can understand ... me as you ... do."

"That is because I love you," he said. "I love you as I never thought it possible to love any woman."

She felt herself quiver at his words and because she was still shy of him she blushed and her eyes fell before his.

"When did you first know that you ... loved me?" she asked.

It was the question every woman has asked the man she loves since the beginning of time.

"I loved you from the moment we met in Monk's Wood," he replied. "You were so different to anyone I had ever known before. It was not only your beauty, my sweet, which beguiled me, but the things you said."

"You mean when we talked at the Look-out?" Syringa asked.

"And when you revealed to me the secret of the ruined Chapel and spoke of Judith as you did, I knew I could never forget you."

"But you ... tried?"

"Yes, I tried," he acknowledged. "I told myself there was no room in my life for a young, unsophisticated girl. I had sworn not to be married. I disliked the idea of being tied.'

There was a pause. Then Syringa said very slowly.

"That night ... when you came to my bed-room ... you meant to ... make love to me."

"Yes, that is true," the Earl admitted. "Circumstances had forced you into my life. I was already bewitched by you, but I was still hanging on desperately to what I believed was my freedom."

Syringa looked down at the table, her fingers playing absent-mindedly with a silver spoon.

"I am very ... ignorant about these ... things," she said hardly above a whisper, "but why ... did you not ... stay with ... me?"

"Because, my darling," the Earl replied, "I could not besmirch anything so pure, so perfect. When I went back to my own room I knew I not only desired you, but loved you as a man can love only once and for eternity. Because of that love, I had to give you a chance."

"A ... chance?" Syringa questioned.

"A chance to be sure you really loved me. I knew how narrow and restricted your life had been. You had met so few men. How could you be sure – as I was – that we were meant for one another?"

"Supposing I had wished to marry ... someone else like ... the Marquis?"

"Then I should have lost you," the Earl said simply. "But it was a gamble I had to take for my own peace of mind."

"And ... now?"

"I will take no more risks with my happiness or yours, my beloved."

He saw the glory in Syringa's eyes and then she said hesitatingly :

"I do not ... want you to be ... disappointed in me because I am so ... ignorant. Will you ... explain to me ... about making love?"

There was a small silence.

"In a little while you shall learn about love," the Earl replied in a deep voice. "But, my dearest heart, I would not frighten or shock you."

"You could ... never do ... that," she answered.

She saw a sudden glint of fire in his eyes.

Then he rose from the table and started to snuff out the candles.

While they had been eating and drinking the sun had sunk below the horizon, and now the sky was dark with the soft purple and blue of a summer's night.

"Where are we going?" Syringa asked.

"Upstairs," the Earl answered.

"To see the Dome?" she exclaimed. "I would like that!"

He led her across the tiled floor by the light of one candle which he held in his hand.

When they reached the bottom of a carved marble staircase, he blew it out and she went ahead of him up the stairs.

She did not know what she expected, but as she stepped through the doorway into the upper part of the building Syringa gave a cry of astonishment.

The room was lit with huge candles set in high gold candlesticks.

Here there were no windows, but the walls were decorated with very different murals from the ones downstairs.

All the birds to be found in Monk's Wood encircled the room.

There were the green tits, the little brown sparrows, the blackbirds and starlings, the speckled thrush, the blue-winged jay and black and white magpies.

There were also brilliant butterflies fluttering over wild roses, bees seeking pollen from golden honeysuckle and dragonflies hovering on their transparent wings.

Below them were arranged real flowers, lilies, tuberoses, carnations and night-scented stocks, making a bower of blossoms and scenting the whole atmosphere with their fragrance.

Against the North wall there was a huge couch-like bed with a carved head-board exquisitely painted in the Florentine fashion with flowers.

But the ceiling, instead of the curved Dome which Syringa had expected, was covered with blue silk in the deep Madonna blue of the Italian paintings.

She looked at the Earl as if for an explanation.

"I want to show you my last surprise," he said, "and to see it as it should be seen, will you lie against the pillows and look up?"

Surprised, but ready to do anything he asked, Syringa seated herself on the bed.

As if she knew he expected it, she took off her little satin slippers and lifted her feet onto the Italian silk brocade of the cover. Then she lay back against the lace-edged pillows.

"Are you comfortable?" the Earl asked.

"I am so excited," Syringa replied. "I did not believe that an Observatory could be so beautiful and the flowers make it almost like..."

"...our Secret Place," the Earl interposed.

She smiled up at him and he hesitated for a moment as if he wished to take her in his arms.

Then resolutely he went towards the candles snuffing them out one by one.

It was very hot and as the Earl went round the other side of the bed where there were three more great candles, he drew off his close-fitting blue satin coat and threw it down on a chair.

His shirt was of very fine muslin, his white cravat, meticulously tied, was of the same material.

"He is so handsome ... so strong ... so very much a man," Syringa thought to herself.

Then she blushed because the very masculinity of him made her shy.

The Earl started to blow out the last of the candles, and as he did so Syringa saw that hanging from the ceiling at the side of the bed was a thick silken cord finished with a tassel, rather like a bell-pull.

As the last candle went out she saw the Earl reach up to pull the cord.

Slowly the Madonna blue silk of the roof slid back and

now Syringa with her head back on the pillows could look up at the heavens.

The sky was bright with stars and the light from a nearly full moon flooded into the room filling it with a mystical silvery light.

It was so breath-takingly lovely that for a moment she could find no words in which to acclaim it.

Then as she stared upwards feeling she had never seen anything so unique or so wonderful, she found the Earl was on the bed beside her looking down at her.

His face was in the shadows, but his head and shoulders were silhouetted against the moonlight.

She felt a thrill run through her because he was so near, and the sweet rapture of it made her breathless.

"Now you ... really look ... like ... Jupiter," she said almost incoherently.

"And can I lift you up to the sky so that we forget the world and be aware only of ourselves and our love?" he asked.

"You remember ... that was what ... I said."

"I remember everything you have ever said to me," he answered.

"And you have arranged ... all this for ... me?"

"For us both," he said, "so that we shall never forget our wedding-day, never forget that from now on that whatever we do we do it together. Will that make you happy, my beloved?"

Syringa drew a deep breath and then she whispered:

"I think I ... understand now what Mama ... meant when she told me only to ... give myself to ... a man I loved with ... all my heart."

"You love me like that?" the Earl asked.

"I love you with ... all my heart ... my body ... and my soul. I love you with ... all of me. And I want you to tell me ... how I can give you ... myself."

She reached up her arms as she spoke to put them round his neck and draw his head down to hers.

215

"My darling, my love, my wife!"

His lips passionate, insistent, demanding, held her captive, she felt his hands touching her, his heart pounding against hers.

Then Syringa knew that he lifted her towards the stars and there was nothing in the whole Universe save themselves and their love.

OTHER BOOKS BY BARBARA CARTLAND:

*Romantic Novels*, over 95, the most recent published being :
A Virgin in Paris
Love to the Rescue
Love is Contraband
The Enchanting Evil
The Unknown Heart
The Secret Fear
The Reluctant Bride
The Pretty Horse-Breakers
The Audacious Adventuress
Lost Enchantment
Halo for the Devil
The Irresistible Buck
The Complacent Wife
The Odious Duke
The Wicked Marquis
The Little Adventure
The Daring Deception
No Darkness for Love
Lessons in Love
Journey to Paradise


*Autobiographical and Biographical:*
The Isthmus Years 1919–1939
The Years of Opportunity 1939–1945
I Search for Rainbows 1945–1966
We Danced All Night 1919–1929
Ronald Cartland (with a foreword by Sir Winston Churchill)
Polly, My Wonderful Mother

*Historical:*
Bewitching Women
The Outrageous Queen (The Story of Queen Christina of Sweden)
The Scandalous Life of King Carol
The Private Life of King Charles II
The Private Life of Elizabeth, Empress of Austria
Josephine, Empress of France
Diane de Poitiers
Metternich – the Passionate Diplomat


*Sociology:*
You in the Home
The Fascinating Forties
Marriage for Moderns
Be Vivid, Be Vital
Love, Life and Sex
Look Lovely, Be Lovely
Vitamins for Vitality
Husbands and Wives
Etiquette
The Many Facets of Love
Sex and the Teenager
The Book of Charm
Living Together
Woman – the Enigma
The Youth Secret
The Magic of Honey
    Barbara Cartland's Health Food Cookery Book
    Barbara Cartland's Book of Beauty and Health
        Men Are Wonderful


*Editor of:*
The Common Problem, By Ronald Cartland (with a preface by the Rt. Hon. The Earl of Selborne, P.C.)

*Drama:*
Blood Money
French Dressing

*Philosophy:*
Touch the Stars

*Radio Operetta:*
The Rose and the Violet (Music by Mark Lubbock). Performed in 1942

*Radio Play:*
The Caged Bird: An Episode in the life of Elizabeth, Empress of Austria. Performed in 1957

*Verse:*
Lines on Life and Love

# Susan Howatch

**PENMARRIC**          50p

The magnificent bestseller of the passionate loves and hatreds of a Cornish family.

'Grippingly readable' – THE SUNDAY TIMES

'A fascinating saga . . . has all the right dramatic and romantic ingredients'
          – WOMAN'S JOURNAL

**CALL IN THE NIGHT**        30p

Claire Sullivan comes halfway around the world to answer a desperate cry for help from her sister, Gina. But when she arrives in Paris, Gina has disappeared . . .

Susan Howatch 'knows how to spin a colourful story' – WOMAN'S JOURNAL

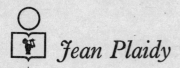

*Jean Plaidy*

### THE THREE CROWNS          35p

Born leader and brilliant soldier, William of Orange thought the English court a hotbed of vice and conspiracy – Charles II with his mistresses, the Dukes of Monmouth and York ambitious for the throne.

William wanted no reluctant bride, but the three crowns of England, Scotland and Ireland were worth a little sacrifice. He would marry the fifteen-year-old Mary, bring her back to Holland, and teach her who was master . . .

All England rejoiced. Only Mary wept. She knew married people were rarely happy . . .

*Elizabeth Byrd*

**THE FLOWERS OF THE FOREST** 30p

Edinburgh in the year 1513 – a city of riches and of squalor. This is the setting of this bold and colourful novel, which follows the fortunes of two women . . . Bess Andersen, a spirited country girl who turns prostitute, and Margaret Tudor, the English princess who becomes James IV's Queen . . .

**IMMORTAL QUEEN** (Mary Queen of Scots) 40p

A chill morning in the Great Hall at Fotheringay, February 8th, 1587. Elegant and still beautiful, an anointed Queen prepares to die as bravely as she had lived . . .

'A joy to read' – DAILY EXPRESS

# *Georgette Heyer*

**FALSE COLOURS**                                    35p

When Kit Fancot returned from Vienna to his
mother's town house, he little thought that the
following evening would see him masquerading
as Evelyn, his identical twin brother, and calling upon Evelyn's fiancée, the Hon. Cressida
Stavely.

This delightful Regency story, sparkling with
wit and romance in the best Heyer tradition,
proves devilishly captivating!

'With Georgette Heyer you don't buy a book,
you buy a world. If it suits you, you settle
down forever' – TIME MAGAZINE

# *Madeleine Brent*

TREGARON'S DAUGHTER          35p

The excitements of that summer's day in the
early 1900s begin a chain of adventures which
sweep the lovely Cadi Tregaron from fisher-
man's cottage in Cornwall to stately home in
Kent to the mist-shrouded canals in Venice.

'One of the best romantic thrillers I have read
in years' – ANNABEL

'Extremely well done with imaginative and
surprising twists' – WOMAN'S JOURNAL

These and other PAN Books are obtainable
from all booksellers and newsagents. If you
have any difficulty please send purchase price
plus 7p postage to PO Box 11, Falmouth,
Cornwall.
While every effort is made to keep prices low
it is sometimes necessary to increase prices at
short notice. PAN Books reserve the right to
show new retail prices on covers which may
differ from those advertised in the text or
elsewhere.